"What pirate wouldn't want to ravage you, looking like that?" Jane hooked her thumbs in her wide leather sash with a possessive leer.

Renee took the one step necessary to lift her lover's hands from the belt. Smiling, she surveyed Jane's costume. "You look marvelous in breeches. And that shirt, all that muslin."

"Arrr!" Jane wiggled her hips. "It's not me breeches you'll be wantin', lass, but what's under 'em!"

"Oh, no hokey accents."

"Avast! What yonder wench stiffens me resolve?"

"I've never heard it called a resolve before," Renee quipped. Torn between laughter and wanting to wrap her hand around what she knew Jane had on under the breeches, she turned back to the mirror, uncharacteristically flustered.

Jane was behind her again, with another of those soft, loving kisses on the nape of her neck. "Are you sure, sweetheart? We don't have to go through with it."

Meeting Jane's gaze in the mirror, Renee said firmly, "I am absolutely sure. I've always wanted to do this."

18TH
AND
CASTRO

KARIN KALLMAKER

Bella
BOOKS

2006

Bella Books, Inc.
P.O. Box 10543
Tallahassee, FL 32302

Printed in the United States of America on acid-free paper
First Edition

Editor: Anna Chinappi
Cover designer: Sandy Knowles

ISBN 1-59493-066-X

*For Maria, with a special nod to the Great Pumpkin
and all the wonderful things that go bump in the night.*

Eighteen but refusing to grow up

About the Author

Karin's first crush on a woman was the local librarian. Just remembering the pencil through the loose, attractive bun makes her warm. Maybe it was the librarian's influence, but for whatever reason, at sixteen Karin fell into the arms of her first and only sweetheart.

There's a certain symmetry to the fact that ten years later, after seeing the film *Desert Hearts*, her sweetheart descended on the Berkeley Public Library to find some of "those" books. The books found there were the encouragement Karin needed to forget the so-called "mainstream" and spin her first romance for lesbians. That manuscript became her first novel, *In Every Port*.

The happily-ever-after couple now lives in the San Francisco Bay area and became Mom and Moogie to Kelson in 1995 and Eleanor in 1997. They celebrate their twenty-ninth anniversary in 2006.

All of Karin's work can now be found at Bella Books. Details and background about her novels and her other pen name, Laura Adams, can be found at www.kallmaker.com.

Contents

Up on the Rooftop

~Part 1~

"If we time it just right, we can get in." The dare in Suze's eyes makes my heart pound.

"But we'll get in trouble." I hate that I whine, but I've grown to hate even more that something as simple as sneaking into an apartment building is the wildest thing I've done in a decade.

"The view from the roof is great. You can see the whole street. You brought binoculars, right?"

"Sort of."

"What does that mean? Oh, look—here!" She bolts across the sidewalk, catching the building door just before it closes behind a tenant who exited.

I slither in behind her, and she makes a show of patting her pockets for supposed keys on the way to the elevator. On the fourth floor we climb up one flight of stairs and exit onto the roof.

"There will be other people later, but they'll assume we belong or are someone's guest. Especially if we stay quiet." She slings her backpack against the wall and leans over. "Come and look, Amy."

I set down my satchel and timidly peer at the street below. At first I'm a little dizzy, but when I realize I can see all the way from Market Street on my right to Nineteenth on my left, a span of nearly three blocks, I'm thrilled. "Last year it was so crowded I left. This will be great."

"What brought you out last year?" Suze looks perfectly innocent but I'm well aware that she's fishing for some kind of declaration from me—she's been doing that since she was hired in our department.

"I'd only been here a few weeks, and it was the biggest event since I'd arrived. Everyone says that the guys have the most amazing costumes. In Cedar Rapids, believe me, the most outrageous thing you can do on Halloween is fishnets and a black wig."

"There they are!" Suze pulls sleek binoculars from her backpack. "Well, believe me, that's going to seem tame the moment the sun goes down. And by midnight, Cedar Rapids will seem a long, long way from here."

Why San Francisco, Amy? That was the question all my relatives and friends had asked. Yes, it's expensive to live here. Yes, they have crime and foreign food. Yes, jobs can go up in smoke. None of them had asked the same question Suze had been dancing around since we'd struck up a friendship at work. *You're going to San Francisco because you're gay, right?*

"See the building across the street?" Suze points and I nod as I open my satchel. When the sun goes down it's going to be cold. "Last year, let's just say, there were some inspiring indoor activities."

"You mean . . . ?"

"Oh, yeah. Wouldn't I love to have an apartment in that place? Right in the heart of the Castro, and—oh look!" Suze points down. "I think she lives in that building. I'm pretty sure I watched her last year. Look at those boots."

I am looking. Is that the kind of woman that turns Suze on? I

4

don't glance down at my comfortable Hush Puppies, nor finger my cloth jacket. "I don't think I could carry off all that leather."

"Do you want to?"

Something in Suze's voice suddenly makes my heart pound. I can't look at her. "Not really. I don't think that's me."

"Neither do I." Her voice makes me think of velvet. "I like you just as you are."

Don't look, I tell myself. I don't know why I am so scared. I have been desperate for her to touch me for at least six weeks, yet irrationally afraid I won't survive if she does. Yes, I'm gay, I'd wanted to tell everyone at home. There was just one technicality—I'd never been with a woman. I want to be with Suze, though.

I set my hoodie next to my feet and scrabble in my satchel.

"Are those *opera* glasses?" Suze is openly laughing at me, something I am used to from her.

"Yes." I can finally glance in her direction again. "Got a problem with that? They're all I had."

Sometimes Suze has a wit that can cut glass. Her first few weeks on the job as a programmer she'd occasionally scourged me—clothes, hair, being from the Midwest, you name it. I told myself maybe her behavior was the same thing as a playground punch to the arm, and given the way she was looking at me now, maybe I'd been right.

Her eyes are soft and yet still dancing with laughter as she reaches into her backpack. "I brought a pair for you in case you forgot. These should work better."

I accept the binoculars and reach into my satchel again. "I brought beer."

Her grin deepens. "Perfect."

We clink bottles and take a long draft. Planting our elbows on the top of the wall, we settle in to wait for sunset.

Brand New Woman

~ 2C ~

"It doesn't fit anymore." Nancy studied her silhouette in the mirror and said a bad word under her breath.

From the depths of the closet, Brenda announced, "The last time you wore it was two kids ago."

"Like I don't know that," Nancy said to her reflection. Could her underwear be any more utilitarian? Whitey and definitely not tighty. "I can't go out like this. Look at my boobs!"

The peasant blouse clung so snugly that all the pulling in the world didn't cover more than half her breast. She couldn't even bring herself to try on the broadcloth skirt.

Brenda finally came out of the closet, still in her robe, a velvet cape in one hand. "Oh my."

"See what I mean?"

"Why, yes, I certainly do." She draped the cape on the chair as she paused behind Nancy at the dressing table. "You look delicious." She kissed the back of Nancy's neck.

"I don't mind if you think so, but I don't want half the Castro taking a long look."

Brenda didn't seem to be listening. Her kisses continued across Nancy's shoulder and then around to her chest. "Simply delicious."

"What are we going to do about my costume?" She giggled as Brenda tripped on the vanity stool. "Enough of that."

"No way. Your parents have the kids, and I don't care if we're late to the party."

"Brenda . . ." Nancy couldn't help a shiver as Brenda pulled on the elasticized neckline of the blouse.

"God, you're gorgeous. It seems like forever since we had so much time to ourselves." Brenda pulled one last time on the neckline, and Nancy caught her breath as Brenda's warm, agile tongue licked at a newly exposed nipple.

"I—you—Brenda, we don't have time . . ."

"Yes, we do. Let's go to bed and get comfortable."

Nancy wanted to say yes but found herself squirming out of Brenda's grasp. "I don't know . . . I'm not really in the mood."

"Yes, you are." Brenda rubbed her teeth against the erect nipple she'd been licking. "I'm so glad you're done breastfeeding."

"My nipples will never be the same shape."

"Like I care. I'm just glad I'm not sharing anymore." Brenda paused in her adoration to look up at Nancy seriously. "I'm glad your body is all mine again. I wasn't jealous of the babies, you know that, but I missed you. I missed everything."

"They sag." Nancy looked down as she shifted uncomfortably in Brenda's arms.

"So you're not twenty-five anymore, and you've got two kids. Something is going to change, eventually."

She knew Brenda meant well, but she felt a rush of annoyance. "I don't feel very attractive at the moment."

"You're kidding, right?"

Risking a glance at Brenda, Nancy shook her head. "I sag *everywhere*. My belly's gone to hell. Nothing's the way it was."

"Honey . . ." Brenda crouched at Nancy's feet, regarding her seriously. "Do you think I'm not going to want you or something?"

She covered up her bare breasts as she shrugged. "I don't know why you would."

"How about because I have always found you attractive and I still do?"

To her surprise, Nancy felt the sting of tears. "I stopped breastfeeding three months ago and nothing fits. My slacks, my skirts—even my pantyhose. I swear pregnancy hormones made my legs shorter and my arms longer. I feel like a gorilla and don't you dare laugh!"

There was no sign of amusement in Brenda's eyes, and Nancy felt another rush of tears. "Ignore me, I'm a mess," she managed to choke out before dissolving into sobs.

She let Brenda pull her gently to the bed and had a good cry while Brenda cuddled her. Finally, she muttered into Brenda's armpit, "Hormones. Bloody, useless hormones."

"No," Brenda said quietly. "Well, maybe. But it's not like you don't have reason to be frustrated and upset. Your body *has* changed. We wanted kids, sure, but here you are afterward with sags and bags, and I don't have a stretch mark on me."

"That's not it," Nancy protested, though partly it was. Brenda looked exactly the same as she had five years ago, just as slender and graceful. "I thought the sleep deprivation and gray hair was the worst of it."

"I'm sorry I can't share the changes," Brenda said quietly, "but they only make you more beautiful to me."

"Sweet talker." Nancy wiped her eyes on Brenda's shirt.

"Uh-uh. No, I mean that, honey." Brenda shifted so she could look into Nancy's eyes. "You are more beautiful than ever, lush and soft and curvy. Every time I look at you I am so glad I'm a dyke."

"You're very sweet to me."

"Hey," Brenda said, her eyes going murky. "Do you really think I'm so shallow that just because your body changes I don't want you anymore?"

11

"No—"

Brenda pushed Nancy onto her back, her hands firm. "Do you think I make love to you because of how you look?"

Nancy gasped as Brenda's knees pushed her legs apart. "No—"

"I touch you because it makes both of us feel good. God, honey, I fuck you because of the sounds you make." Brenda's hand was suddenly between Nancy's legs, and Nancy couldn't help a reflexive moan, deep in her chest. "That sound. I love that sound."

"Brenda—" Nancy tried to say more but a series of fierce, demanding kisses stopped all the words, and the play of Brenda's fingers under the elastic of her undies was making it increasingly difficult to think.

"I want you naked. I love your skin and the way it makes my hands tingle." Brenda yanked at Nancy's clothes, baring hips and stomach and breasts. "I want to devour you."

"Oh, baby!" Nancy made herself hold back tears, not sure if it was fear or confusion or frustration that she could not believe Brenda wasn't just being nice.

"Do you remember that weekend at the beach? That night we never slept?"

"Yes," Nancy murmured against Brenda's demanding mouth. *When I was thinner, younger and everything was tighter?*

"I fucked you all night because of the moans and the wet and the way you cried when it was so good. I fucked you all night because touching you got me soaked, and I couldn't get enough. Remember?"

"Vividly," Nancy whispered. She watched Brenda shrug out of the robe and shivered as they melted together, naked skin against naked skin.

"You excite me. You always have." Brenda bit Nancy's index finger, then licked her palm. Pulling firmly, she guided Nancy's hand down her body. "Feel me. Feel how hot you get me."

Nancy was stunned by the slippery wet that ran over her hand. "Oh, baby, you *are* hot, aren't you?"

Brenda's growl was an answer as she bit down on Nancy's nipple. Her hips jerked in response to a flutter of Nancy's fingers. "Please, baby, this is what you do to me."

She loved the feel of Brenda's full lips and the way they curled and parted. Brenda tightened around her fingers as she slipped inside, and suddenly Nancy felt twenty-five and falling in love with a woman for the first time. Feeling a woman, Brenda, for the first time.

"Right there," she whispered. "Yeah . . . right there." A surge of sensuous power flowed from her fingertips as she stroked Brenda exactly the way that made her gasp and close her eyes.

Through trembling lips, Brenda murmured, "Nan, yes." Her eyes opened and Nancy felt Brenda's fingers slipping into her. "Let's do this together."

"Uh-uh." Nancy pushed harder into Brenda even though Brenda's touch was sending tingles into places that hadn't tingled in quite a while. "You. I want to fuck you. Fuck you good, baby."

Brenda gave a strangled cry and had to put both hands back on the bed to keep her balance as Nancy pushed in again, harder.

"Like that, oh, you're so wet." Brenda's excitement left Nancy's thigh coated and slick as Nancy grinned in fierce pleasure. Brenda's first tremor of climax pulsed against her fingers. Then the tender, responsive flesh seemed to explode with wetness as Brenda shuddered.

"Oh Nan, oh Nan . . ."

Of all things, it was laughter that bubbled up inside her when Brenda collapsed on the bed next to her. "God, that felt just wonderful," she said as she cupped Brenda's face.

"You're telling me."

Nancy smiled into a slow, loving kiss. For a few minutes

Brenda seemed incapable of doing anything but that, which pleased Nancy even more.

Finally, Brenda stretched with a little laugh. "That really was wonderful, but it's not all I want."

Though greatly reduced, Nancy still felt a tickle of anxiety as Brenda lazily feathered her fingertips down Nancy's torso. Stretch marks, the emergency C-section scar and the occasional thick black hair that grew back faster than she could pluck it—how could Brenda find any of that sexy?

Her reverie was broken by the shrill of the bell for the apartment downstairs, audible, as usual, through the thin floor. "Hope she's home or that racket will drive me nuts."

"What racket? There's no racket." Brenda nibbled along Nancy's jaw. "I could touch you all night."

You *did* turn her on, Nancy told herself. She was as wet as she has ever been for you. She put her fingers to her nose and inhaled Brenda's heady scent. Something stirred, and she recognized it belatedly as excitement blended with yearning. She wanted Brenda's touch. But she also wanted Brenda to want her, the way her body was now.

"Can I make a confession?" Brenda planted a series of small kisses across Nancy's chest.

Nancy smiled indulgently. "What?"

"I feel pretty lucky here. I mean, you have changed. It's like I get to be with a new woman and yet she's still my wife. Fooling around without fooling around. And this new babe . . ." Brenda stretched to kiss Nancy on the mouth. "She's really hot. Makes me dizzy. I can't wait to make love to her."

"You like her stretch marks?" She said it as a joke as she mulled over Brenda's confession.

"I like her tummy and all the ripples in her skin. They're interesting to touch. Like they're teasing my fingers."

"What about her ass? Looks kinda big to me."

Brenda slid between Nancy's legs, nudging them open with

14

her knees. "Her ass is a crime in motion." She slid her hands under Nancy's hips, cupping the full cheeks. "I don't think I'm going to lose my grip when I fuck her."

Nancy couldn't help the gasp that escaped her. Brenda's voice was edged with raw desire. Everything Brenda did was turning her on.

"Oh yeah," Brenda whispered. "Some things are familiar. When she gets hot, her nipples get hard, just like this."

"God, Bren." Nancy arched her back as Brenda bit down gently. Her nipples were larger than before and as they stiffened, Nancy was aware of a different, but equally pleasurable prickle that seemed to connect directly to her clit. "God, that feels good."

"I'm just getting started." With a slow grind, Brenda moved her pelvis against Nancy's. "She seems to like my approach."

Her mouth dry, Nancy said, "I think she does."

"The new babe, she's very responsive," Brenda murmured. Nancy couldn't help but move in rhythm to Brenda's slow, subtle dance. "I think she's going to like the way I fuck her."

Another gasp escaped Nancy as she shuddered. "Yes, baby. I think she will."

"She likes it when I tell her how hard I'm going to fuck her."

"Bren . . ."

"She likes to get hot and high and make me work."

"Please, Bren."

"She likes to beg."

"Oh, baby, baby please."

"Is that what you want?"

Nancy's legs trembled as she felt Brenda's hand cupping her cunt. "Yes. You know I do."

"You're wet." Brenda kissed her hard. "Wet and hot, and you feel so good."

A long, fervent moan filled Nancy's head as Brenda slipped inside her. Brenda had always known how to turn up the heat and those strong, sure fingers immediately found and caressed her G-spot.

"Good lord, baby—things *have* changed. I used to have to reach for it." Brenda pushed Nancy's legs open wider. "But now it's right . . . there. Feel that?"

"Oh, fuck." A hard tremor raced the length of Nancy's spine. "Oh, Bren . . . damn . . . Don't stop."

Brenda's grin was fierce. "Right under the tip of my index finger . . . all I have to do is push. Circle it—oh, yeah, now you're wet. Come on, baby."

Brenda clamped her free hand onto Nancy's hip, holding her down. Nancy was again aware that things felt different, but everything that needed to feel, to be stroked, was responding. She was completely open to Brenda's touch. Her eyes filled with tears, and her mouth was no longer dry. Wet, she was so wet. She felt like a river flowing onto Brenda's hand.

"Are you going to scream for me? Scream while I fuck you? You want more? Or should I stop?"

Nancy locked her gaze with Brenda's. "Don't you dare stop."

"Scream for me, baby."

"Fuck me!"

"I *am* fucking you, baby!"

Brenda went deep and Nancy felt a hard jolt of near-climax. Her body arched from the bed, and she froze in place while Brenda continued to fuck her. Muscles wanted to melt, but she was too tight now, caught at almost.

Brenda shifted her hand. "It's right there, right under my fingers. God, I can practically lick it."

The touch of Brenda's mouth to her clit sent a shock wave through Nancy. "God, oh yeah, like that!"

For those rich, rare moments, the world went away. There was nothing but starlight bursting on the inside of her eyelids and the waves of release. Melting, she was melting, tears mixing with laughter as Brenda let her fall back to the bed. Gasping for breath, she closed her eyes and held on to the sheets.

16

From below them someone said, very loudly, "I wonder if they're going to fuck some more?"

Brenda giggled as she wiggled her fingers inside Nancy. "Shall we?"

"Damn thin floors," Nancy muttered. "There's no privacy in this place."

"Stop thinking," Brenda said. She flicked Nancy's clit with her tongue. "More coming. This time I want you to soak me."

"Didn't I?" Brenda's tongue was amazingly agile, and Nancy resisted an urge to purr.

"Okay, so I'm greedy."

"Oh, baby, that feels so good. We're going to be late to the party."

"Let's skip it and have a party here." Brenda's tongue parted Nancy's folds, slipping around, through, over and finally in.

Nancy sank her fingers into Brenda's hair. "Okay," she said with a shudder. "Let's party right here . . . right now, baby. Right there."

Wrapped tight in Brenda's arms, Nancy tuned out the bedlam that was happening just below their window. The street was jammed with San Francisco's best partygoers, and the celebration would last until nearly dawn.

Last year at this time her second pregnancy was starting to show. Nancy sought out the stretch marks that marked her abdomen, fingering them in the dark.

Brenda murmured something in her sleep and shifted so their legs were tangled. The bed smelled downright funky now. More laundry tomorrow. *Isn't there always laundry after the ecstasy?*

Considering all that she felt for and with Brenda, what was a little laundry to complain about? Thinking of her family and all that the future promised, Nancy smoothed her fingers over the stretch marks and for the first time didn't wish them away.

Borrowed Plumage

~1C~

Her headache already pounding to match the noise from upstairs, Carmen snatched open the door. "Took you long enough!"

"Hey." Fyre looked Carmen up and down. "Who's doing who a favor?"

"Sorry." Carmen backed out of the doorway. "Come on in. I've got a headache, that's all."

Fyre carefully set down the zippered garment bag she'd been carrying in the crook of her arm. "You better take care of these. They were my first set."

"I'll be too nervous to do anything that might hurt them. ¿Cerveza?"

"Sure, if you're having one." Fyre followed Carmen to the tiny kitchen. "What's that noise?"

"You should hear it from the bedroom."

"Really?" Fyre twisted the top off her beer and sauntered in the direction of the rhythmic creaking and dim but unmistakable sounds of passion. "Somebody is starting early."

"For a while nothing happened up there. The kids are noisy enough, but it looks like they're back to form. Before the first kid I couldn't think some nights for them going at it."

Over their heads a voice screamed, "Fuck me!" followed by a guttural, "I *am* fucking you, baby!"

Fyre laughed. "Well, they'll be busy a while."

"Tell me about it. It's the most action this room has seen in forever."

Fyre regarded her with the outright disdain only an old friend could be permitted. "How long are you going to do this celibacy thing? Cori isn't coming back. If she did, I'd have to beat the crap out of her, so either way, she's not coming back."

Carmen rubbed her throbbing temples. "I don't want her back. I don't want anybody."

"Oh, so that's why you're borrowing my leathers for Halloween dress-up?"

The creaking and thumping above them abruptly stopped. Carmen stared at the ceiling. It was too good to be true.

Fyre opened her mouth, but just as she did the noise resumed with a hoarse, "God, oh yeah, like that!"

"What did you say?" Carmen headed for the bathroom. Pills, she needed pills for her head.

"I said," Fyre shouted, "you can hear everything they're doing!"

Carmen winced. "Why are you yelling?"

The pace above them slowed and the voices were low for a moment.

Fyre rolled her eyes. She bellowed back, "I wonder if they're going to fuck some more?"

There were giggles above them and the bed began creaking again, more slowly, and the voices were definitely quieter.

"There," Fyre said in a normal voice. "Now they know the floors are thin."

"I think it's just this apartment and that one with the paper floors. The building used to be a big boarding house, and this was the common room, double high ceiling. So they chopped it into pieces and put the ceiling-floor in for that apartment, but there's got to be no insulation." Carmen tossed back three tablets and returned the bottle of ibuprofen to the cabinet. "The party down the hall will be loud, but at least the doors and walls are thick."

"And they've never heard you doing anything loud?"

"Get off my back, Fyre. If I ever met anyone who turned me on, I might. But after Cori I just don't want to get burned again."

"Maybe tonight you'll meet someone."

"Let's see the costume." Carmen tried to put a smile on her face. She was wishing she'd never had the inspiration of a free costume in the form of Fyre's leathers. She didn't want to go out tonight. It would be noisy and crowded and pointless. She could pop into the party in 1A, say hi, and get an early night.

"It's not a costume." Fyre unzipped the garment bag. "These are real. I wore them for years before it was time for a new pair."

"I know that. I rode bitch at Pride three years ago, remember?"

"How could I forget? I was the only one whose passenger had her shirt on."

Tears stung her eyes. Apparently, criticism was all Fyre was going dish out tonight. "I only meant that it's a costume to me. I couldn't be more vanilla."

Fyre held up the jacket and pants. "You're going to look hot."

"I'm going to look like a femme who stole a butch's outfit." She took the jacket from Fyre and tentatively inhaled the rich aroma of the soft, well-loved leather. There was something sensual about it, to be sure, but it had never turned her on the way it obviously did others.

"I personally think there are few things sexier than a femme dressed up butch. Marlene Dietrich—yowza."

"I don't even know why I'm doing this. Just because a bunch of people at work will want to know what I wore and if I say I didn't go out I'll get those looks." Carmen glanced at Fyre.

"That look, thanks so much. It's great to get pity looks from friends too."

"I don't understand why you live in the Castro if you're not going to *live* in the Castro."

"Maybe because it's a half-block from the MUNI station? Twenty minutes to work? I don't need a car?" Carmen sighed heavily. "Just because I live in the Castro doesn't mean I fuck anything that moves. Nearly every other apartment in this building is occupied by a couple."

Fyre glanced meaningfully at the ceiling. "At least they're having sex."

"So I'm not a card-carrying lesbian anymore if I'm choosing a little celibacy?"

One hand on her hip, Fyre said drily, "If I thought it was a choice I'd leave you alone. You never called Cindi back. She thought you were hot-on-a-stick. You'd be having sex if you wanted to."

Carmen chewed hard on her lower lip. "Maybe that's the whole point, Fyre. Maybe I don't want to have sex right now."

"You used to be—"

"I was a lot of things before Cori."

"Fine. You do whatever you want, Carmen. Stay in, go out, get laid or read some smut and do yourself. Just don't get anything on my leathers, okay?" Fyre drained her beer. "I need to run. Dara will have my head if I'm late back."

"Who are you tonight?"

"Robin Hood. Dara's refused to be Maid Marian. Again."

"That's the trouble with falling for another butch, isn't it? Dara will never dress up femme—no more than you would. So you can just stop asking."

"I know. She said she'd only be Marian this year if I promised to be the femme next year."

"You'd be a great Marie Antoinette."

24

Scandalized, Fyre snapped, "Fuck that noise. So she's Will Scarlet. I'm in green, she's in red."

"You'll both look great in tights." Carmen found herself grinning at Fyre, who was pouting. The beer and pills were both helping her mood, and she knew better than to let Fyre's caustic tongue get her down.

"We'll look like little Christmas elves." Fyre took her leave, still muttering about the problem of costumes for two women with such similar tastes in clothes.

Alone, finally, Carmen looked at the jacket, pants and gloves on the sofa, and realized her first dilemma was what to wear under it. She'd seen Fyre in a white tee, black tee and nothing at all. But Fyre was an A cup. Carmen glanced down at her chest. She wasn't sure she'd be able to zip the jacket over the Girls.

A shower cleared her head even more and by the time she put on a bra and her preferred lacy boy shorts, she was ready for the adventure of the leather.

She stepped into the form fitting pants with confidence. She and Fyre had traded jeans on campouts with no problems. She had the pants halfway up when she realized that a pantyhose approach was going to work better. Halfway up the second time she reached for moisturizer. When she finally pulled up the invisible zipper on one hip she felt as if she was going to baste on the inside. Good lord, she'd seen Fyre wear these on hundred-degree days and not bat an eye. Her body temperature was already climbing.

"Well," she announced to the mirror. "It's a sure bet nobody's ever worn a lace bra under this jacket." Given how bitchy Fyre had been earlier, it felt decidedly like payback to defile the inside of a butch's jacket with Victoria's Secret.

After she slipped her arms into the sleeves, she ran the zipper up to just past the front hook in her bra. She'd forgotten a T-shirt, but her reflection told her she looked just fine without one. Of course, if the zipper came down at all she'd be flashing people. Hell, it was Halloween. Why not show off the assets?

She fingered the wide lapels and heavy snaps. Leather really wasn't her thing, but she had to admit she liked the way the outfit made her feel larger, but at the same time sleek, trimmed to nothing but the essentials. All she needed was her black hiking boots and she'd look like every other woman in the Castro. Well, except for lipstick and eyeliner. Huh. Maybe she should take off the makeup.

Thirty minutes later, after gobbling a nutrition bar and finishing her beer, Carmen stepped out onto the street. The sun hadn't quite set, but the shadows were rising in the Castro. The pastiche of old-fashioned and modern storefronts was slowly fading into the dark while a growing press of bodies filled the blocked off streets.

The makeup had stayed on. Carmen was well aware that anyone who looked close would figure out she was wearing borrowed plumage but she felt unnatural without something on her face. She didn't belong in this heavy leather jacket, but it was a costume, she told herself.

She spent an hour just crowd-watching as disco music blared from the bars. There was character homage in plenty, with roving troupes dressed as the full casts of Friends, Seinfeld— well, those were the two she recognized. Batman and Robin were popular again this year, as were Xena and Gabrielle. She saw several others she had no way of identifying, which made her feel unhip and old. What was an O.C.? If she didn't know did it mean she had to turn in her lesbian card?

It's not like you're having lesbian sex, either, she chided herself. Fyre is right—your credentials are really thin these days. Work, sleep, work, sleep. Not exactly the high life of a San Francisco lesbian.

But was this her choice? Jostled by a group pausing to pose for photographs, she realized that even in her heavy butch leathers she was in the minority. *The only party in months you've gone to is mostly for the boys.*

You're not in a party mood, she told herself, and it's been a couple of years since you were. She decided on a fancy coffee for a treat to carry home with her and ducked down Seventeenth where the lines might be shorter. It wasn't her favorite shop, but there were only a half-dozen waiting to order. The tables were crowded with women, and she felt more at home. The boys could have the streets and the girls were obviously parked in the coffeehouses. Costumes ranged from Veronica Lake to generic gypsies and black cats. There were plenty of women in ordinary street clothes too.

She finally reached the front of the line and ordered her frothy favorite, complete with whipped cream. The conversations in the room were boisterous and upbeat and she selectively tuned into them for something more interesting to consider than her own morose musings.

"I just think it's so retro, and not in a good way," one woman was informing her table of companions. "I think labels are forcing us all to conform to someone else's idea of what we're supposed to be."

"Oh, I don't know. Just saying we're lesbians is using a label." Carmen lost the rest of the rejoinder as she accepted her tall, hot drink and stepped over to the condiment table to add chocolate and fake sugar.

"It was a *really* hot book," drifted from a table on her right.

"I hate reading—it's too slow. I'd rather watch TV."

"Not like anything but books really reflect our lives."

"Every story in there was about femmes loving butch cock."

Carmen surreptitiously glanced at the table occupants. The ensemble group of gangsters and floozies was nearly finished with their drinks.

"What's wrong with that? Those are my favorite stories," one floozy offered.

27

Increasingly agitated, the gangster pushed her fedora back. "It's not the only way to be, you know?"

The floozy laughed. "Of course not. There's on top, on the bottom, on the floor." She slipped one hand over the thigh of the gangster next to her. "I do love butch cock."

"Butch cock!" The gangster got to her feet with a clatter. "Whatever happened to butch pussy?"

The café went quiet, then the red-faced gangster grabbed her plastic machine gun and fled. A few moments later one of the floozies went after her.

"What's got into her?"

Carmen stirred her coffee. She caught the eye of a brush-cut butch near the window and they exchanged what-the-hell shrugs. Obviously, dyke drama had changed in the years since she'd been hanging out. In the years since Cori.

Sipping her coffee, she slipped out into the crowded street again, avoiding ostrich feathers, a wiener supported by five guys marching to "Hail to the Chief" and a leather daddy with two slaves on a leash. Unlike hers, their costumes, complete with studded collars and clanking chains, did not look borrowed. It wasn't as if she didn't occasionally fantasize about the edgier aspects of sex and power, but that was so very much not her scene.

Yeah, so, what is, Carmen? She felt like an idiot walking around in leather and reflecting on her own nonexistent sex life. At least other people were having sex, regardless if it was what she liked or not. Before Cori she had liked sex, liked it a lot. Cori had truly fucked her over with that dominant psycho tailspin.

First Fyre, and then the brouhaha in the coffeehouse had upset her. Butch cock? Butch pussy? What about just being who you are and doing what you liked? Did everything have to be about power and gender-fucking and pain?

As if, Carmen told herself with a sigh, you've put anything

into action except your vibrator since Cori. So Cori was screwing someone on the side—a lot of someones. So Cori had thought she could bring that secret dominatrix life out into the open with you and hadn't waited around for a little thing like consent. So Cori tried to have you arrested when you'd kicked her ass, literally, out the door.

What a sad, pathetic scene it had all been. The apathy of the cops to Cori's complaint had played in Carmen's favor—but it had also rankled at the same time. If Cori had succeeded in beating Carmen up, in the name of some hot, rough sex, they'd have not cared about that either.

She paused to look in the window of her favorite card shop. The store was far too crowded for her to enjoy browsing and her coffee was nearly done. She was already tired of the endless jostling and there seemed little point to being a spectator at a street party where everyone else's gaiety was highlighting her own lack.

When she trudged up the short flight of stairs from the lobby to the first floor, she heard the commotion of the party in 1A. Neenah and Ace would be offended if she didn't show. Just a few more minutes and she could get out of this ridiculous outfit.

"Girlfriend! You look unbelievably hot!" Neenah's embrace at the door was bone-crushing.

"I'm sweating like you wouldn't believe."

"Not that kind of hot." Neenah stepped back, her head tipped to one side. "You should go for leather more often."

"It's a costume, believe me. I am about as opposite a leather dyke as one can get."

"Who cares?" Ace sidled up behind Neenah. "Just looking at you is giving me ideas about what I'm gonna do to Neenah later."

Neenah slapped playfully at Ace's roaming hand. "You are so bad!"

Obviously, Neenah and Ace—and the couple who lived upstairs—had never heard of lesbian bed death, Carmen thought, as she kept up her end of the conversation. It was early yet, for the party at least, and only a dozen or so women were hanging out. Ace had chosen retro Halloween music for the background, and Carmen was pretty sure if she stayed long enough, she'd hear Bobby Pickett and the Crypt-Kickers more than once.

"Hey, come and meet Joyce. She's just transferred onto my shift at the hospital." Ace dragged Carmen toward a tall woman swathed in brightly colored skirts and a shimmering blouse that deliberately left one shoulder bare.

Ace performed introductions, made several suggestive leers, then hurried away to answer the door. She heartily embraced a scantily clad black cat and high-fived a diddy-bopping James Dean. The cat's skirt was short enough to reveal the tops of her fishnet stockings.

"And I thought the leather was uncomfortable." Carmen tried not to feel the trickle of sweat running down her spine.

"She looks like that outfit is a second skin. I was never that much of a girl," Joyce admitted. "Though it looks great on you, why don't you take that jacket off?"

"I can't. I mean, it's not that kind of party." She glanced down meaningfully at her chest.

"Oh, I didn't realize." Joyce ran a lazy hand through tousled blond curls, and Carmen became aware of her soft drawl. "I'm sure somewhere in the Castro tonight there is that kind of party."

"Then I'd feel about as out of place as I do in these clothes." Carmen sipped her beer, trying to decide if she thought Joyce was interesting or not. She had a very pretty smile and a silky voice.

Waving a hand at her own gypsy outfit, Joyce said, "I'm not exactly a gypsy type either, but it was cheap."

Carmen laughed. "This is all borrowed too. How are you not a gypsy type?"

"Oh, I'm too boring. My friends complain I'm harder to get out of my apartment than kudzu out of a Louisiana garden. I'm just a homebody."

"I know what you mean." Carmen sipped her beer and found it easier to look Joyce in the eye. "So you're a nurse, like Ace?"

"I never wanted to be anything else. What do you do?"

"Computer geek."

They chatted for a while about Ace, then the pros and cons of their jobs, and Carmen was surprised to find herself enjoying the banter. When a trickle of sweat finally broke free of her hairline, she mopped at it, certain it was unattractive. "I suppose I could go home and change."

Joyce looked alarmed. "You'll come back, won't you?"

"Yeah, I'm just down the hall, kitty-cornered. On the other side of the vacant apartment."

"Oh, good. I'm dreadful at parties and it's nice to find someone fun to talk to."

"Me, too, yes, I mean." She found herself studying Joyce's brown eyes and the continuing rise in her body temperature wasn't all due to the leather. She was suddenly aware that Joyce was studying her as well, and Carmen couldn't stop staring at Joyce's mouth.

Joyce said abruptly, "I'm sorry, I have a thing about leather. I don't suppose you'd let me wear the jacket."

"I really can't take it off here." Goodness, Joyce's lips were what she was sure some poet would term kissable.

Joyce gave a little start, then blushed. "No, I suppose not."

Carmen toyed with the snaps on the sleeves. If she really were a leather dyke, wouldn't she be inviting Joyce back to her place to wear the jacket? But she wasn't. It wasn't her at all. "You could try it on at my place."

Her lips parted, Joyce breathed out, "I could."

31

What did I just do? Carmen put her beer down, hoping her shaking hands didn't show. "We'll be right back," she said to Neenah on the way out. "Joyce wants to, uh—"

"I have a leather fetish and Carmen is going to let me play with her jacket."

"Well, that's a new one," Neenah joked back. "Don't do anything I wouldn't do."

In the hallway Joyce whispered, "According to Ace, there isn't much Neenah won't do."

"Ace is a braggart of the first order. They're as vanilla as I am," Carmen said over her shoulder. At the top of the stairs she sidestepped a stocky woman in street clothes who obviously wore more under her jeans than her boxers. She carried a small overnight bag that seemed heavier than it looked as she continued up the stairs to the second floor. A second glance jostled Carmen's memory—Carrie? No, Claire. Claire had lived upstairs for a while with Jeneen, but a year or so ago Terra had moved in and Carmen hadn't seen Claire since. Carmen wondered, for just a moment, if Terra knew Jeneen's ex was dropping by, dressed for action.

Not that it was any of her business, she told herself. She unlocked her door, flipped on the lights and stepped back to let Joyce in. She felt a little faint.

Joyce waited until they were standing awkwardly in the little space behind the closed door to say, "Looking at you in that outfit, it's hard to believe you're vanilla."

She's taller than I am, was all Carmen could think. She'd never kissed anyone taller than she was, though why she was focusing on that was beyond her. Joyce would think she was daft. "It's not like I've had a lot of practice lately."

"Me neither."

The silence that fell tingled all around Carmen's ears.

"So . . ." Joyce finally said.

"The jacket." What you ought to do, Carmen told herself, is go into the bedroom and take it off. Put on a ratty old T-shirt, a chastity belt, and bring the jacket out to her. "Do you want to take it off me?"

"God . . ." The sharply indrawn breath made Carmen even more aware of Joyce's curvy, tanned bare shoulder. "I can't believe I'm doing this."

Shock and raw lust spun in her head as Carmen watched Joyce's fingers close on the zipper pull. For a moment she thought she heard her upstairs neighbors going at it again, but realized it was her fantasy of the sounds she wanted to make with Joyce, right now.

Maybe she really liked leather after all.

The low burr of the zipper sent a shiver along the backs of Carmen's knees. She heard Joyce catch her breath.

"Oh, look at you." Joyce left the zipper most of the way down and one fingertip trailed over the hollow between Carmen's breasts. "Not at all what I expected under such a butch jacket. Can I take this off of you too?"

The moan that escaped Carmen sounded like it came from someone else. It was deep and needy and ready. Joyce's finger coiled around the clasp that kept Carmen's lacy bra closed. "In a while," Carmen murmured. "You wanted the jacket, didn't you?"

"That's not all I want." Joyce leaned close and a very small part of Carmen felt a wave of relief that the several inches between their heights were no impediment at all to a good kiss. The rest of her got lost in that kiss and the sensation of Joyce's tongue parting her lips.

It felt wonderful. Carmen fancied she could hear an unlatching lock for every year since she'd been kissed like this releasing in her brain, springing open in response to Joyce's tongue, her cologne.

33

She kissed Joyce back with a fever in her mouth. Joyce's fingers were at the jacket zipper again, and then Carmen felt blessed cool air across her shoulders.

She stepped back with a gasp and Joyce's gaze was on her with a greedy edge. She wanted to strip both of them naked and wake up all the neighbors. "I think," she said as steadily as she could manage, "you should try the jacket on."

Joyce finally looked down at the garment in her hands. "Sorry, I was distracted. You're beautiful."

Carmen was starting to love that soft drawl. "I think you should try it on the same way I was wearing it."

"Does that mean you want me to take my blouse off?"

Carmen moved closer to Joyce again, wondering where her courage was coming from. "No, I mean that I want to take your blouse off."

A flush rose along Joyce's neck. "I thought you were vanilla."

Surprised, Carmen answered, "I am."

"You sounded, right then . . . like . . ."

"Hmm? Like what?"

"Like a top." The flush deepened to an outright blush.

"Do you want me to be a top?" It was getting too complicated, Carmen thought. She didn't want to be a top or a bottom or a middle. She just wanted to be who she was. Sometimes aggressive. Sometimes putty. The butterflies in her stomach stopped fluttering.

"Do you want me to be a bottom?"

They stared at each other for a long minute, then Carmen swallowed hard. If it was the wrong thing to say, so be it. "I just want to go to bed with you. Can't it be that simple?"

Joyce let out a long sigh. "As long as we both get . . . what we need."

"Just tell me." Carmen unbuttoned Joyce's blouse and couldn't help a little smile as the butterflies came back in full force. "Do you like oral sex?"

"Giving and getting, yes."

She slipped the blouse off of Joyce's other shoulder and took a deep, steadying breath. "Do you like . . ."

"Like what?" Joyce shook the blouse down her arms.

Don't be a teenager, Carmen told herself. Just say it. "Do you like fucking? Getting fucked?"

"Oh, yeah."

The blouse dropped below Joyce's breasts, and Carmen felt a fool for not realizing that of course Joyce was wearing no bra. Her nipples were plump and rising in that tantalizing way that made Carmen's mouth water. She was certain if she nibbled them they'd get large and stiff.

Joyce met Carmen's gaze with a directness that took Carmen's breath away. "I like being fucked, I like fucking, I like orgasms and doing things more than once."

"I think," Carmen said with an attempt at a smile, "we'll both get what we need, then."

Joyce drew on the jacket, never taking her gaze from Carmen's face. Carmen could see a flicker of heightened arousal in Joyce's eyes. Her lips seemed to grow more full and the pulse in her throat jumped.

Brushing Joyce's fingers away, Carmen joined the zipper and pulled it up until Joyce's breasts were framed by the opening. "That's gorgeous on you."

Joyce began to raise the zipper higher, but Carmen again brushed her fingers away. "No. Leave it like that."

The next kiss drew them into a tight embrace, and it seemed natural to lean Joyce into the door and gently pin her shoulders there. Some time later, when Carmen gasped for breath, she realized that Joyce had undone her skirts and the colorful fabric was pooled around their ankles. Joyce's black panties gleamed like silk, and Carmen wanted to explore them with her mouth.

Maybe it was the leather, but gazing into Joyce's glistening, eager eyes, Carmen felt a surge of confidence. With a slow smile, she reached into the jacket to cup Joyce's breasts, then molded them while pushing the jacket opening back so that it framed and supported the beautiful fullness. "Like that—the perfect way for you to wear this jacket."

Joyce said hoarsely, "It's making me feel really slutty."

"Is that bad?"

"No . . ." Joyce groaned as Carmen brushed both prominent nipples with her thumbs. "I don't get this way, normally. That's all."

"I think I like you this way. And believe me, I will have my slutty moments."

Joyce fumbled with the clasp on Carmen's bra. "No fair that you are still covered up."

She normally didn't think of herself as slutty, but when her naked breasts pressed into Joyce's, and the zipper on the jacket abraded her nipples ever so slightly, Carmen was willing to admit to *wanton*. She wanted sex, wanted to feel good and wanted Joyce moaning into her mouth while they kissed.

She pushed her thigh between Joyce's, and they moved together in a slow, sensuous dance.

"God, I love leather. This is incredible. I'm wearing it and you're wearing it and your leg feels fantastic."

"I really want to go to bed," Carmen said. "That means taking it off."

"As long as I get to help." Joyce smiled into a kiss.

In the bedroom, Carmen admitted shyly, "I really am a little rusty." She leaned down to turn on the small bedside lamp.

Joyce had moved directly behind her, but Carmen was still startled by the possessive caress of Joyce's hand across her backside. "These pants are wicked on you."

She thrust back because it felt so incredibly good. She wasn't some romantic fool thinking a hot one-nighter was anything more than just that. Without having to worry about if such admissions were good for "the relationship" she said throatily, "I like that."

"Oh, so do I. Your ass feels fantastic, and I swear . . ." Joyce's hand drifted lower, and Carmen didn't hold back a moan. "I can feel all of you through it."

Fyre would kill her if she got the pants stained, Carmen thought, but at the moment she didn't care. The leather blunted the intensity of Joyce's caress, but when Joyce pressed in, the sensation rippled outward with a wave of heat. She made a noise of pure lust as she spread her legs a little more and bent further to put her forearms on the bed.

"Oh . . ." Joyce put her other hand on the small of Carmen's back. "Oh, that feels so good. You're so wet and I can feel everything."

It had been so long since anyone had touched her that part of Carmen wasn't surprised that her clit was so swollen. Joyce was leaning into her now, and the feel of the jacket framing Joyce's full breasts, all pressing down on her naked back was so sensual that Carmen groaned.

"I want to . . ." Joyce shifted so she could roll Carmen over. Dizzied, Carmen gazed at Joyce in the low light, her pulse pounding.

"You look so unbelievably hot like that." Joyce's black panties were now plastered to her and gleaming. The leather jacket still framed her breasts and her nipples were as large and prominent as Carmen had thought they might be. She arched up to take one in her mouth and Joyce groaned.

"I swear," Joyce said shakily. "There's an aphrodisiac in leather fumes."

"You could be right." Carmen flicked her tongue against the plump nipple, finding the texture and taste yet another turn on.

"I want to . . ." Joyce pressed Carmen back onto the bed and slowly went to her knees next to it. Then she pushed her face between Carmen's legs, hard.

"Oh, *¡dios! Madre de—*" Carmen sucked in a lungful of air only to let it out in a long, loud groan. If the neighbors upstairs heard her, she did not care in the least. She wound her fingers into Joyce's short curls. Through the leather and panties—how could it feel so good?

Joyce was moaning into Carmen's crotch, her mouth running up and down the seam of the supple leather. Carmen draped her legs over Joyce's shoulders while one hand fumbled with the side zipper. When she was able, she pushed the pants down, then Joyce grabbed and pulled.

Carmen shifted so that Joyce could pull again, and they succeeded in getting the pants down to Carmen's hips.

"God, you smell good!" Joyce yanked Carmen's panties down just enough to make room for her mouth.

At the insistent push of Joyce's tongue Carmen felt a sharp clenching that stunned her. Cori, with all her insistence on mind games and role playing, had never gotten her this high, this fast. Joyce was sucking at her with little moans, and they were both panting and writhing. She had to come, she needed to now.

Joyce's muffled "so unbelievably good" followed by a fluttering push that parted Carmen's lips all the way to her opening was the final trigger. Carmen screamed and clutched Joyce's hair as she bucked against the ravenous, relentless mouth. So good, *fantástico, sí, sí* . . .

"I wish," Joyce said a few minutes later, "that I understood Spanish."

Carmen realized she was still holding Joyce's hair clenched in her fingers. She loosened her grip, then cupped the side of Joyce's face. "I said that was fantastic. And it was."

"I didn't realize I could get so focused. I wanted you in my mouth, and that was all there was to it." Joyce glanced up and Carmen fondly returned the shy smile.

"Your knees must be killing you."

"I hadn't noticed, but now that you mention it . . ." Joyce rose a little stiffly to her feet, but Carmen quickly pulled her down on the bed.

"I think we're discovering a few new things. Want to go back to the party?"

Joyce shook her head, and then kissed Carmen very, very thoroughly. The taste of her sex on Joyce's lips was another aphrodisiac.

I'm going to have to get everything dry cleaned, anyway, she thought. "Let's stay here, then. You can wear the pants next, if you want to."

Joyce laughed. "How did you know I was going to ask?"

Though it seemed a riskier question than any she'd asked so far, Carmen was glad she didn't sound hesitant. "Stay for breakfast?"

"I'd like that," Joyce said.

They kissed again, and Joyce melted into her. Carmen decided that after breakfast she'd suggest a shower. They'd wash off the smell of leather and sex and see if they still couldn't keep their hands off each other.

And if the leather turned out to be necessary, she'd ask Fyre if she'd be willing to sell.

For the Last Time

~2B~

I rang the bell of my old apartment, not liking that I was the visitor.

The overnight bag was just heavy enough that I was calling myself a fool for having packed both the bag and my jeans. I knew what Jeneen liked and pleasing her was something I *still* yearned to do, and that was the whole problem.

Terra opened the door, all granola and sweet. She didn't look the least bit like she'd send her girlfriend's ex an e-mail requesting a house call for sexual purposes. I have to admit my first thought was "bad joke."

There was no sign of Jeneen in the living room and for a moment, I once again thought this was some kind of prank. "So."

Terra bit her lip. "I really thought you'd back out."

"This is purely for your research, isn't it?" I wasn't about to tell Terra my reasons for agreeing. I think she knew and that was bad enough.

"Did you bring a white lab coat, then?"

"I packed only what I know Jeneen likes." I sauntered past Terra after she stepped aside, aware that Terra couldn't miss the fact that I was loaded for action.

I had no idea what her deal was. Did she think toys were anti-female, penetration aping heterosexuality, or did she not know how to use one? She sculpted with clay, so it wasn't as if she was afraid of getting her hands messy. Jeneen really enjoyed a few specific things and, hell, even if strapping something on wasn't Terra's favorite thing, she could hold one in her hand, couldn't she? Why did that idea escape so many women?

Damn it, I don't know why I'm here. I should leave.

I heard the little click the bedroom door always made, and Jeneen appeared.

That's why I'm here, I told myself. I loved her, I always would love her, and Terra's plan let me be with her, one more time. Maybe one more time with me would change Jeneen's mind about who she wanted in her life.

"Hi, Claire." Jeneen stayed near the bedroom door. She was wearing an old silk kimono I'd given her when we'd first started dating. I wondered if Terra knew that.

"Hi." We hadn't spoken in at least six months. I guess you could say I was a little bit angry she'd asked me to leave. I'd never understood what she meant by "I need more than this." I tried not to look smug. Apparently, whatever "more" she got with Terra wasn't enough. "So this is really okay with you?"

"It was Terra's idea—"

"But is it okay with you?"

She pressed her lips together, and I remembered that interrupting her was on the list of things she did not like about me. "After she and I talked about it, yes."

So we were going to be serious and clinical, were we?

Turning to Terra, I said clearly, "I'm going to fuck her senseless."

They both gasped. Terra looked momentarily pained, but it wasn't as if I cared how she felt. Jeneen looked startled and damn, yeah, she was turned on. I could feel sex adrenaline pumping in my blood, too, the way it had always pumped for her. The day I moved out we'd gone to bed twice. We'd still met up every couple of weeks for several months. She always said it was for the last time, but it never was, not until Terra showed up in her life.

"Are you ready to see her in that condition?" When Terra didn't answer, I said to Jeneen, "Are you okay with her seeing you the way we both know you can be?"

She gave me a level look. "I want to be that way with her, so yes, I'm comfortable with it. I *need* her to see it, to believe it."

Terra finally spoke. "I just can't bring myself to . . . hurt her."

I couldn't help but bristle. "I've never hurt her. Hard is not the same as hurt. That's not what it's about."

"I've tried to tell Terra that, but—"

"Let's show her." I'd interrupted Jeneen again, but I was here to fuck her. And while she didn't like me cutting her off over dinner, it was a different matter in the bedroom. I was anxious and pissed off to be the visitor, but looking at her had me tight and ready. I couldn't wait to get lost in her.

Nobody had to show me the way, and I smiled at the sight of lit candles and the neatly turned down bed. Terra's handiwork, no doubt. However, I was topping this scene—that's what she had suggested, wasn't it? That I show her how to properly top her girlfriend?

It mystified me, really, because Jeneen had never been shy or made me guess. She wasn't complicated, either. I could have written Terra back and just said, "Hold her down and fuck her hard for a long time," and that would have been the whole truth.

The last time I was with Jeneen, I didn't know I'd never be with her again. The chance to try one more time, to remind her of all the really good things we'd shared, that was why I had instead written back, "Are you suggesting you want to watch me with Jeneen?"

Terra could watch—she didn't exist for me.

I blew out the candles after turning on the bright overhead light, and pulled the covers completely off the bed. I liked lots of light. I liked watching Jeneen come. There was a handy stack of towels on the floor. "Trash bags?"

Jeneen appeared in the bedroom doorway with the package in her hand. Terra looked mystified. Good lord, hadn't she made Jeneen come properly in all this time? No wonder I was here. There was a time just looking at her the right way would get Jeneen's panties soaked. From moment one, we'd been flammable around each other.

I took the box from Jeneen and pointed at the chair. "Sit there while I get ready."

Draping one unfolded trash bag over the edge of the bed, I covered it with a soft towel, then glanced at Jeneen. She was watching and imagining why I'd want some protection there, which was exactly what I wanted her to do.

I put another on the floor below the first, covered by another towel, then lined the middle and other side of the bed with several more. Mattress protection could not be taken too seriously, not when Jeneen was really turned on.

Terra was openly skeptical. "You're kidding."

"Well, that's enough for the first hour or so," I answered. "We'll get fresh ones after a while." I could tell she thought I was just showing off. To Jeneen I firmly said, "Come here."

When we were eye-to-eye she took a deep breath, and her breasts brushed my denim shirt. My own were swelling, and the bedroom narrowed to her, me and the bed.

Without touching her, I asked, "How are you feeling tonight, baby?"

A shiver washed over her, and I saw lights flare in those lovely green eyes of hers. "I'm feeling very yes tonight."

I slipped off my denim shirt, revealing the ribbed A-line tank

46

that she'd always liked on me. "Good. I need all the yes you can give me."

It was easy to undo the tie on her robe, and she was naked underneath. I wanted to close my eyes and breathe in the mixture of scents that equaled Jeneen for me: her shampoo, soap, the delicate cologne and the subtle but unmistakable scent of her cunt. All of her was going right to my head and I wanted to melt and hold her close. By the time we were done, I told myself, she'd let me hold her.

Her lips parted as I looked at her, then I saw her gaze dart to Terra. I cupped her chin with my hand and said quietly, "There's just me. And this."

I put her hand on my cock and reveled in the shudder that ran the length of her body. "Oh, Claire."

"I'm going to take care of you." I pulled her body to me and kissed her throat and the line of her jaw.

Jeneen sighed quietly. "It was always easy, wasn't it?"

"Yes, baby. Very easy."

Moving quietly, Terra sat down in the chair Jeneen had vacated. It would shortly be out of Jeneen's line of sight, which was fine with me.

Slowly, Jeneen wrapped one arm around my neck. "Have me, Claire. I want to do everything tonight. I've been thinking about what it's like to be with you all day. For days."

I'd longed to hear her say just that, all the months I hadn't talked to her. I was too proud to be her lap dog, and I wasn't going to be her butch on the side, either. All of me or none of me. Tonight, she was getting it all.

The green of her eyes grew deeper when I undid the first button on my jeans. Then I put her hand on my crotch. "Take out my cock."

I fondled her with increasing roughness, relishing her firm ass cheeks as I squeezed them, then smoothed the satin of her

47

arms. She was panting, just a little, by the time she got my pants open. She took my cock in her hand and weighed it without looking down. "My favorite?"

"Let's see." I kissed her deeply, then spun her toward the bed. "Get ready to feel it."

She dropped the kimono before she bent over, and I paused for one short moment to enjoy the curve of her body as she rested her elbows on the bed. I lightly brushed my fingers over her cunt, and found her deliciously wet. Still, I opened the overnight bag that I'd tucked just under the bed and set a bottle of lube on the bedside table after pumping a liberal amount onto my hand.

Leaning into her, I loved sliding my hand up and down my cock. It never felt so natural and so right as when I was fucking Jeneen with it. I nudged her ankles farther apart, then squeezed her cunt possessively. "Say yes, baby."

"God, Claire. Yes. Fuck me."

I teased her opening with the head. "What do you think? Is it your favorite?"

She arched back, pushing herself several inches down my cock. Sounding as if she was gritting her teeth, she said, "Yes, damn it. Fuck me with it."

We both moaned when I sank into her the rest of the way. I was delirious with the smell of her. And the sounds she made, those greedy, hungry, animal sounds—I loved those, too. We were really starting to move, the way we'd always moved, easy and fast.

I resisted the urge to look over my shoulder and ask Terra if she could see her girlfriend enjoying a good fuck, finally. I didn't like the woman—I had no idea what Jeneen saw in her. But I wasn't fucking Jeneen like this, so good and wet, to pay Terra back. It wasn't about Terra. I loved fucking Jeneen, and I'd thought I'd never get to again.

She was shoving back to take me as I gripped her shoulders to give her what she wanted. It was hot and hard and fierce, and I could feel her first climax building. "Is this what you need?"

"Yes. Yes, I need it." She buried her face between her forearms. "Give me everything."

"You've got it all, baby. Like *that*. And like *that*. Gonna come for me? Get me all wet?"

Her head came up, and I felt the spasms rock through her pelvis. She was abruptly too tight to fuck and I froze, stunned by the way I could feel her muscles clamping down on me. It had always amazed me. She was the first and only woman who'd ever climaxed just from my cock.

She cried out, and I felt the splash of her hot come soaking my jeans. She wasn't the only woman I'd ever been with who gushed, but Jeneen was by far the most copious. The first time we'd been together I'd told her she was an incredibly fun fuck, and it was still true. How could Terra have not figured this out?

Gasping for breath, she arched her back and pushed up onto her hands. My cock was still buried in her, and I didn't get the impression she wanted it any other way. Reaching under her I found both nipples. A light brush, a sharp pull and we were on again, both of us grunting with each stroke.

I put her on her back, finally, in the middle of the bed, liberally coated both of us with more lube, then dove in. She locked her ankles around my thighs while I clamped my hands onto her upper arms and held her down. And we fucked. We fucked for a long, long time, and she came for me, again and again.

When one towel got too sodden, we moved on to the next. More lube, more fucking. It had always been this easy, the way I could scratch all her itches. The way no one else ever had and the way I didn't think Terra ever could.

We reached a point where Jeneen was nearly exhausted. I gave her water to drink and let her breathe while I did the same.

But when she lazily began stroking my cock I knew she wasn't done. The more I itched the more she had a scratch, and I loved the sexy, desirous look in her eyes.

Just as I was going to push her back into the bed for another fuck, she turned her head toward the chair. "Are you okay, honey?"

I think right then I could have hated her. Her hair was a wreck, her skin mottled with passion, my arms were starting to tremble, and we both reeked of sex. She had my cock in her hand and was asking the woman who hadn't a clue how to fuck her if *she* was okay.

Terra said shakily, "I'm okay. I didn't know you could . . ."

"You have to trust that I know what I want, honey."

Yeah, I wanted to snarl, you want me. I bent my head to the nearest nipple and sucked it sharply into my mouth. She moaned and gave me an open-mouthed look that said she was ready for more.

I wasn't feeling charitable. I didn't want her thinking about Terra, I wanted her thinking only about me. But I wanted Terra to realize she could never take care of Jeneen the way I could. "Why don't you move closer?"

Terra scooted the chair forward slightly.

"No, I mean, why don't you sit here on the bed?" And get a good look at what it takes, because you don't have it.

Jeneen's eyelids drooped the way that meant she was extremely high. She watched Terra take off her sweatshirt, revealing a simple white tee. After a brief hesitation, she stripped off her leggings, then joined us on the bed.

Fine, I thought. Let her feel how hard Jeneen likes it. She'll never be able to match it. Reaching up, I put Terra's hand on Jeneen's breast. "Touch her, just like that, while I fuck her."

Jeneen's moan was throaty and loud. When I started to move inside her again her eyes half rolled back in her head.

"God, baby, you look so beautiful," Terra whispered.

"Don't tell her that," I said fiercely. "Don't tell her sweet shit right now. She needs to get fucked. Tell her she has the hungriest cunt you've ever felt. You have to fuck her, like this. Like this."

Jeneen's moans became a rising keen of pleasure, and she yanked at me, increasing my pace.

What did Jeneen ever get from Terra except herbal tea? I never understood why she left me, I never understood what she wanted from Terra when I could give her *this*, and *this*, and *this*, harder, faster, until she comes and can't stop. "She wants to fuck like an animal, forget the world and get off. You have to keep up and give her everything you've got."

I loved fucking her, loved opening her and taking her, loved driving her crazy by pausing to see her shudder and gasp. "Make her beg for more sometimes."

Jeneen's eyes were unfocused. I watched her nails dig into Terra's arm as Terra tweaked and toyed with her nipple. But when I drove into her again, she chanted, "Claire, *yes*, Claire, *yes*."

Pleased and incredibly turned on, I said to Terra, "Are you watching? Do you see how she really likes it? Not nice and sweet." She'll forget her own name, I wanted to add, but she'll never forget mine.

"Claire, *yes*, Claire, *yes*."

Terra's gaze was riveted on the uninhibited passion etched on Jeneen's face. I wished Jeneen's nails were in my back, marking me so I could see it and feel it for days. We were there, right at the peak where all the veneer of accepted behavior is stripped away, when we were as physical as animals and rising up to a place beyond words.

Terra kissed Jeneen, biting her lower lip. She said something in Jeneen's ear that I couldn't quite catch. Jeneen trembled, and her cunt opened even more to me, and I grunted going into her again.

"Terra, baby, yes. That's what I want, love me, baby."

I wanted to fuck her so hard so she couldn't move without remembering me on top of her. My thighs were burning, my pelvis was raw from shoving into her. We were fucking like there was no tomorrow.

She cooed Terra's name again and then I realized . . .

I realized that for me, there was no tomorrow.

She was sucking on Terra's tongue and her eyes had focused on Terra's face, and I will never fuck her again. Never feel her move like this. It really was the last time.

Jeneen closed her eyes as she let out another deep moan. "Fuckmefuckmefuckme . . ."

Her voice echoed in my head, and I tried to catch it, pin it to a memory I would never lose. I moved faster, harder, sweat trickling down my back. I didn't want her to open her eyes yet and look at me as if she'd forgotten I was the one on top of her.

I wanted her to think only of me, to be capable of nothing else. It was the last time she would be like this, and I wanted it to go on for days.

I fucked her hard and kept her high, shifting the pace just often enough that she couldn't go over the edge and out of my life forever.

Terra breathed out, "God . . ." and I realized she was up against the wall, holding on to Jeneen as I fucked her across the bed. We were all sweating profusely, and Jeneen was crying and moaning with an intensity I'd never heard before.

Terra leaned down again and said just loudly enough for me to hear, "Come, baby. Show me."

Jeneen's hoarse cry told me that she was coming and this would be the last one.

"Open up for me, baby," I said in her other ear. It couldn't be over. "We're not done. Baby, please."

She collapsed, limp and tear-streaked. I pulled out of her and rested back on my haunches, remembering that she liked it when her clit was gently kissed and licked after the sex was really good—the aftershocks settled her.

I was about to bend to take her clit between my lips when Jeneen weakly pushed Terra's head down. "Please, baby. God, Terra, please."

"You're so beautiful," Terra said. "I didn't realize how strong you were. I love you, sweetie."

Jeneen was crying for real, and I didn't know what to do. Terra kissed and soothed her cunt, then her belly, then carefully gathered Jeneen in her arms as if she was fragile.

"What's wrong, sweetie?"

"Nothing," Jeneen gasped. "Except I'm scared you think I'm a dirty little—"

"No, no, sweetie." Terra cuddled her close. "That was amazing. You were beautiful and if it takes me the rest of my life, I'll try to make you feel that way."

I got off the bed before someone thanked me.

What had I thought was going to happen? Why had I done this? Jeneen would never have me in her bed again.

I'd given away the only thing I had that she had ever wanted.

I stripped off the harness and toy and rolled them into my wet jeans. Warm sweats from the overnight bag would get me home. I saw the stupid toothbrush I'd put in at the last moment. Had I really thought we'd sleep three in a bed? Or that Terra would be so awed by my performance that she'd leave?

What kind of fool was I? My legs were shaking. I was utterly drained. I didn't want to go home and never be with her again. But I couldn't stay here and watch Jeneen love Terra.

Love her even though she's not me in bed.

Love her maybe because she's not me the rest of the time.

From the bedroom door I looked back at them, wrapped tight in each other as Terra poured a river of soft, loving words around them both. With me, Jeneen had seemed to like to spend a few minutes talking about what we'd done, and I'd always told her how hot she was and how much I loved fucking until neither of us could move.

Terra was different—*love* and *beautiful* and *female* were the words she was using the most. Sticky sweet words and not at all what I thought . . . Jeneen was only sniffling now. She was smiling, too, obviously sleepy.

Maybe it had been better, not knowing it was for the last time.

"Claire, wait." Jeneen wiped her eyes. "You don't have to leave."

"Yeah, I do. You both got what you wanted."

"What about you? Did you get what you wanted?" Jeneen had that soft after-sex look all over her.

I didn't answer her in anger or simply to pay her back by repeating the meanest thing she'd ever said to me. I said it because I was watching Terra soaking up all that soft adoration, as if Terra had been the one who'd been rocking her very being the whole time.

"No, I didn't," I said slowly. "I need more than this."

It was for the last time. Finally.

Please

~2A~

"Butch cock!" Nat got to her feet with a clatter. "Whatever happened to butch pussy?"

Ash couldn't believe it when Nat ran out of the café. It hadn't been an official date, true, but they were the only two unattached members of their running club, and it had been understood they were "together" for the night. Ash had welcomed the designation even though Nat seemed oblivious to it. Nat, in Ash's unbiased opinion, was thick in the head sometimes.

"I'll go after her," she muttered. There was no way she was being abandoned. Beads swinging, she clutched her tiny handbag and held her flapper bucket hat to her head as she ran out into the night.

Thank goodness for the bright orange tip on Nat's machine gun and the unmistakable cut of her gangster fedora. Ash followed her for half a block, getting stepped on. "Nat! Come on, Nat! I'm wearing heels. Wait up!"

Finally, she caught up to Nat, who had paused in a doorway. She looked sheepish. "I'm sorry. You didn't have to chase me down."

"What was that all about?"

"I don't know." Nat wouldn't look at her.

Ash wanted to stomp her foot. "Right. You just announced that you'd like a woman to appreciate your womanhood from time to time, but you don't know what that outburst was about?"

Nat used the tip of her machine gun to push back her fedora. Nat admitted she was an adrenaline junkie, but Ash thought the ascetic look with the short hair that curled on top was highly attractive. "Okay, so the last five dates I had all wanted me to walk around wearing a damned silly contraption with something that weighed five pounds hanging off it. Every single one of them was a pillow queen too."

Ash could have pointed out that if Nat would stop chatting up women twenty years younger than she was, she might get a different result. Part of her wanted to demand, "What am I, fifty-five-year-old chopped liver?" Instead, she mildly suggested, "You're hanging out in the wrong places, obviously."

"What's the right place?"

Honestly, Nat was thick, thick, thick. "I don't know. Gee, you could think about joining a club or something. You might meet an eligible woman there." Ash didn't add, "Someone your own age who just might like what you like."

Nat sighed. Ash wanted to kick her, and in these stilettos, she could make it hurt too. Whatever did she see in this thick-skulled mushball of a butch?

Fine. So she liked mushball butches.

She watched the parade of bodies outside the little niche where they were sheltered from the ebb and flow of the crowd. "I have to agree with you that it's a whole lot easier to find examples of how butches ought to treat femmes than vice versa."

"I'm more than happy to worship," Nat said passionately. "Pedestal, no pedestal, she wants me to cook and fix stuff, whatever."

"I don't know why you've been single this long, Nat. I mean, yeah, you spent a couple of years letting go of Zoe. She was so special."

Nat put her head down and the rim of her hat shadowed her eyes. "One of the last things she said to me was not to be lonely. I knew she was one-of-a-kind, but . . ."

The flash of a camera opposite them was as brilliant as the light bulb that went off in Ash's head. "Are you looking for another Zoe?"

"I'd love to find someone a little bit like her, yeah."

Ash might have asked, "You mean someone small and femme and feisty, about your age, a terror in bed and truly devoted to making you as happy as you make her? Someone like *me*, maybe?"

Instead, she asked the question that someone as thick-skulled as Nat needed. "Then why are you asking out young women? That last one was twenty-five. She couldn't hold a candle to Zoe. Nobody is ever going to replace Zoe, you know. But certainly none of this last string of women could even come close."

Nat cocked her head and Ash was perfectly aware that if she stepped back even an inch, Nat would bolt again. So she stood her ground. "Honest, Nat. Are you really looking for someone to replace Zoe?"

"No, of course not."

"And so you've gotten exactly what you set out to get, someone not the least like Zoe. What better way to ensure that than to pick up girls who are going to treat you like their personal dildo?"

Nat shifted and Ash remembered that, at least in public, Nat avoided that kind of language—that was what had made her outburst in the café so remarkable. "I see what you're getting at."

"Good. I never had the impression you were a masochist."

"Nah. I don't even play with hurts-so-good."

Ash knew. She and Zoe had traded confidences about their

59

butches from time to time. The whole decade she'd been one half of "Ash and Vic" she'd been well aware that Nat was a wonderful woman. She'd been glad to end things with Vic and Vic's drinking, but of course she hadn't wanted Zoe to die, for heaven's sake. Nevertheless, when she and Nat had both ended up single at the same time she'd subtly put herself in Nat's line of sight.

Too subtly, maybe. The only thing that had made watching Nat with those cute young things bearable had been her certainty that none of them had a clue how to treat a woman like Nat.

Nat shuffled her feet. "Why is it, do you think?"

Ash rubbed her hands over her arms. Nat promptly shrugged out of her jacket and draped it over Ash's shoulders. "Why is what?"

"All the emphasis on butches wanting nothing more than . . . you know, making the femme happy?"

"Girl power gone awry?" Ash shrugged. "I don't know. Lots of things, maybe. I know you remember the days when you and I were pariahs. All we were about, supposedly, was reinforcing that one of us had to be the man. Now . . . in the weirdest way it's like things have come full circle."

"Tell me about it. If you're a butch these days, you're supposed to *want* to be a man."

"It's not that bad. I personally like a butch who looks like a woman."

Nat shadowed her eyes again. "Well, you're the exception to a lot of rules."

"Oh yeah? Like what?" Ash's heart pounded a little harder.

"You never went through a Birkenstock phase."

Her hearty laugh brought a smile to Nat's face. "I'm sorry, I like cute shoes."

"The ones you have on are more than cute."

"Why thank you, kind sir." Ash allowed the slightest of flutters. "I didn't think you'd noticed."

In the dim light of the doorway it was impossible to tell if Nat was blushing, but something in her voice made Ash think that she was. "I've always noticed what you wear. You're a beautiful woman."

Ash was at a loss for words. She knew she was now blushing, too, and wasn't about to admit to the hours it took every week to shape, trim, buff—you name it, she did it. She wasn't going to tell Nat one rotator cuff was sore from overdoing it with the free weights, trying to get just a little more definition in her shoulders so the dress she wore tonight would look as good as possible.

Belatedly, she said, "Thank you. A girl tries."

Nat pulled gently on the lapels of her jacket, still draped around Ash's shoulders. "Are you warm enough?"

"Yes, thank you."

The silence stretched as they both surveyed the crowd again. The reviewing stand was near and many of the revelers in ensemble costumes were gathering together for their portion of the contest. The combination of laughter, music and roaring generators grew deafening.

Leaning close, Nat abruptly said, "So what's your philosophy of how to treat a butch?"

It was a question Ash wanted to answer, in great detail. But she wasn't going to shout it and risk being misunderstood. She cupped a hand to her ear and yelled, "I can't explain it here."

Nat grinned and took her hand. Using her size to clear a path, she pulled Ash along behind her until the crowd thinned slightly. "This is unbearable."

Every café and bar they passed was filled to bursting, and there was no sign of the rest of their club. "I don't think we're going to find anyplace quiet where we can talk."

Nat cut quickly across the street through the gap left between a trio of gorillas on stilts and a platoon of Dorothys clog-dancing in ruby slippers.

Ash realized they were in front of Nat's apartment building.

"I can offer you a brandy upstairs," Nat said.

The light was better, and Ash saw something in Nat's eyes she'd been craving. "That sounds heavenly right now."

Nat let go of her hand as she unlocked the front door. There was a barrage of party noise from an open door just above the lobby. "Neenah and Ace always do a party."

"Do you need to stop in and say hi?"

"No, they know I had a . . ."

Ash preceded Nat up the stairs. "Had a what?"

"A date."

Halfway up the second flight, Ash glanced at Nat over her shoulder. She just smiled and Nat smiled back.

She hadn't been to Nat's since Zoe died, but her recollection told her that Nat had changed a few things. She was relieved by that. Nat's recliner most decidedly faced the television and the curtains were no longer the frilly florals that Zoe had preferred. Instead, simple spare blinds let in slices of moonlight.

Nat switched on the kitchen overheads and Ash followed her, watching her economical moves as she fetched two snifters and twisted open a bottle of *Coeur des Temps*. "I know you like crème de menthe, so I could turn this into a Stinger if you like."

"No, but thank you. Don't do a thing to that XO." She cradled the glass in her hands to warm it and inhaled the aroma, which never failed to make her think of firelight, books and long kisses.

Nat sipped from her glass and Ash watched relaxation steal over her face. From Vic she knew all the signs of alcohol addiction, and Nat's sigh of pleasure had no compulsion to it. For just a while, right after Zoe had died, she'd worried. But once Nat had started showing up for Saturday morning runs with clear eyes and a spring in her step, Ash had let that worry go.

Without saying anything, Nat took her hand and drew her back to the living room. They were seated side-by-side on the couch, within touching distance, before Ash sipped from her snifter.

"Oh my," she breathed after a small swallow. "That's wonderful."

"My favorite. Zoe liked *Courvoisier*, but when that ran out I decided to indulge my own tastes." Almost as an afterthought, she doffed her fedora then ran one hand through the damp curls across her brow. Ash tossed her bucket hat onto the coffee table next to the fedora, liking the picture they made.

"Good for you," Ash said softly. She wanted in the worst way to play with Nat's thick salt-and-pepper hair. "That's as it should be."

"I promise," Nat said abruptly, "not to talk about her all the time."

After another little sip, Ash put her hand on Nat's. "I'd think it odd if you didn't talk about her to a degree."

"You're right about the women. I couldn't even talk to them. A hot date was sex with me and talking on their cell phone."

"Surely all young women aren't that way."

"Probably not. Just the ones looking to get into bed with a dyke daddy."

Ash spluttered into her brandy. "I've never thought of you as a daddy, Nat." She let her gaze openly roam over the unmistakable swell of Nat's breasts. All the running in the world wasn't going to change the fact that Nat still had a bust line supermodels paid for.

Nat took a much longer swallow from her glass, then set it down on the coffee table. Extending her long legs in front of her, she leaned back comfortably into the cushions. "So, what's your philosophy about how a femme should treat a butch?"

Ash eased out of her heels, then curled her legs under her. "Well, first of all, a butch in my life will think she's in charge."

Nat hooted. "Just think it?"

63

"It takes some skill to give her the impression of her masterful control of all she surveys." Ash quirked one eyebrow.

"I'm sure it does."

"A butch in my life will know she's strong and capable, and so am I."

"I have no doubt about that."

"A butch in my life can put me on a pedestal if she likes, but I reserve the right to get off it. I might whine if I break a nail changing a tire, but I will change the tire and then fix the nail."

Nat tangled her fingers with Ash's. "You do have beautiful hands. I like the way you talk with them when you're really excited about something."

Ash found herself once again at a loss for words. She sipped nervously, aware that before long she and Nat would reach the point of a kiss. They'd known each other a long time, and if that first kiss didn't go well, they'd likely not try another. She tried to calm her nerves with one more little sip, then she put her glass down as well. "A butch in my life . . ."

"You're blushing," Nat said softly.

She made a face. "It's the very fine brandy. Besides, a butch in my life will see me blush and hopefully like it."

"I do like it. I like it very much, Ash."

"A butch in my life will know that I'm a lesbian."

"I should hope so!"

"Yeah, well, for all the pillow queens you seem to have found, I've run into a few butches that expect me to be a pillow queen. I know there are lots of different ways to be a lesbian, but the kind of lesbian I am likes . . ." She tightened her grip on Nat's hand. "Not just likes, but *adores* butch pussy."

Nat didn't move. She might not have even been breathing for all Ash could tell.

A slamming window startled them both. Ash realized she'd been holding her breath too. Please, she thought, don't let Nat pretend she didn't hear me.

"I'm not great with words," Nat finally said.

"I've never noticed that."

"Like right now, I can't decide should I tell you that I think you're the most beautiful woman I've seen in years? Or that when I'm around you my palms sweat?"

Ash hoped her smile hid the fact that she was trembling. "You've been hiding your feelings really well."

"I thought you'd think it was inappropriate. You and Zoe were friends. You're a little bit like her in a lot of ways. I didn't want you to think you're a stand-in."

After a hard swallow, Ash said, "You're doing just fine with that word thing. I hadn't realized you felt that way. It's not inappropriate, Nat. Not given that I think we're both attracted and curious. And free to see what happens."

"I want to kiss you."

For an answer, Ash moved a little closer and let Nat's jacket slide off her shoulders. "I'd very much like you to."

Nat didn't take her gaze from Ash's as she leaned in. A shy half-smile warred with longing. The first press of her lips was warm and firm and Ash let out a little sigh.

Nat drew back, then came back for another. Ash's sigh became a moan as their arms found the best way to wind around shoulders and waists. Nat finally pulled Ash fully into her lap and they kissed again. Ash enjoyed the lingering taste of brandy in Nat's mouth, and their tongues began that slow, delicious tangle that suggested other possibilities.

Time seemed to move as slowly as their caresses. Ash was aware only that she was now on her back, and Nat was moving on top of her as they continued those deep, wet kisses. She felt Nat's gentle strength, and it relaxed her more and more. Thoughts of the pleasures they'd both give and receive were growing insistent.

Raising her head, Nat said hoarsely, "Ash, I don't mean this like some teenager, but if we don't stop, I'm not going to be able to."

"I don't want to stop. I want to go to bed with you tonight. I'm aching to make love to you."

Nat moaned, and Ash went to jelly. "Please. Please, Ash."

"What, baby?"

"Please say you mean it. I want you so badly."

"Nat, I'll never *ever* say that to you and not mean it. Let's go to bed."

They kissed their way to the bedroom, losing clothing along the way. Nat opened the blinds in the bedroom. "I love the way you look in the moonlight."

Admiring Nat in black boxer briefs and sports bra, Ash said honestly, "You look awfully good too."

Nat gathered her up for another kiss. "I knew you'd be in lace and garters. It's very attractive."

"I want to be out of the lace and garters before too long."

"Okay." Nat smiled easily and with another long, wet kiss, she eased Ash onto the bed. "You are positively edible."

Ash slithered one hand between them, feeling faint at the heat between Nat's legs. "I'd say the same about you. Please, Nat. I'm dying to taste you."

Nat shuddered as Ash's fingertips pressed into her pussy through the boxers. "Oh, that feels so good."

Ash gave Nat a little shove with the shoulder that didn't hurt, but Nat didn't budge. "Honey, please. Roll over, okay?"

Nat's expression was caught between arousal and a grin. "It's safe to say that I'm always going to roll over for you."

Relaxing into their shared laughter, Ash asked, "Is there any place you don't like to be touched?"

Her smile fading, Nat peeled off her sport bra. She caressed Ash's cheek, then pulled her gently down to her breast. "I like being touched everywhere. Please."

Ash bit back the word *beautiful*. Nat was muscled and lean and strong and absolutely hot. She could say *fabulous* and *sexy* and even *gorgeous*, but no butch she'd ever met thought *beautiful* applied. Nat was beautifully butch, though.

"Incredible," she breathed, running her hands over Nat's arms and stomach. Briefly closing her eyes, she dipped her head to take one lush nipple into her mouth and she was rewarded by a sharp groan from Nat.

"Your mouth feels wonderful."

Ash settled between Nat's legs, liking the way their bodies fit. She continued her adoration of Nat's breasts, hoping she wasn't being overly attentive. They were firm and round and soft and oh, so tastable. She bit down just a little on one nipple, then flicked the tip with her tongue.

"Ash, please."

"I'm sorry, was it too much?"

"No, but please."

Ash stretched up to kiss Nat on the lips. "Yes, lover. Yes, Nat." She flicked Nat's lips with her tongue. "Your clit is next."

Nat trembled as Ash kissed her way down the long, taut body. "Please, baby. God, please go down on me."

"Yes," Ash breathed. "Yes," she said again as she inhaled the intoxicating scent of Nat's pussy. She slipped the boxers down to kiss Nat's mons, then pushed them low enough that Nat could wiggle out of them.

She loved a butch naked, loved it when they wanted and needed and weren't afraid to let her see it. Sensuous power surged through her as her tongue parted Nat's soaked labia. Her butch needed to be loved and if it took all night, Ash would love her.

Sweet and full. Nat's thick wetness seemed to welcome Ash's tongue. It exploded into her mouth, smeared over her chin and cheeks. To Ash, this was what it meant to be a lesbian, to like the taste and texture of a woman's sex. She sucked Nat's labia into her mouth, loving how they curled and played around her tongue. Nat's hard, pert clit was positively wearing a party hat and waving noisemakers. Oh yes, Ash thought, we'll have quite a celebration tonight.

She pushed both hands under Nat's ass, tilting her just a little so she could enjoy all of her. Licking from opening to clit and back again, she heard the rising song of Nat's moaning and felt another surge of sensuous power. Nat was loving every moment, and Ash was going to take her time.

She played, flicked, teased and went back to persistent sucking. Nat's hands were suddenly there, holding her lips open and Ash pressed in harder, capturing Nat's clit with her lips.

"God, Ash, oh—almost. Don't stop. Almost . . ."

Nat's legs abruptly clenched around her, holding her in place as Nat arched up against Ash's mouth. Her hips jerked a half-dozen times while Ash held on, laving the shuddering clit with her tongue. She didn't stop until Nat went completely limp.

"Oh, Ash." Nat sniffed and Ash quickly moved up to take Nat into her arms.

"What, sweetheart?"

"It's just—that was wonderful. You make me feel like hearts and valentines and moonlight."

Ash kissed away the tears at the corners of Nat's eyes. Yes, indeed, she loved a butch mushball.

"I love the way I smell on your face," Nat admitted.

"Good. I intend to smell like this as often as you'll let me."

"Oh, wow."

"What?"

"I felt that—things got all tingly again."

"Really?" Ash propped up on her stronger shoulder. She whispered seductively, "Do you want me to go down on you again? I'd love to."

Nat blushed. "Not right now, but hold that thought."

"Believe me, I've been holding that thought for quite a while."

They kissed, slow and sensuous, then Nat said, "I've been holding a few thoughts about you, you know."

"Really? Like what?" Ash gasped as Nat pushed her thighs apart.

"I've been thinking about femme pussy."

Ash's laugh was lost in another gasp as Nat's hand cupped her entire sex. "All butches think about femme pussy."

"Well, I've been specifically thinking about yours. Would you like me to show you how?"

Ash nodded. "Please."

Human Female
Pon Farr
~3B~

"You think this is fun? To have some kind of human female pon farr every twenty-eight days?" Jax shook off Tate's embrace.

"Well, honey, I'd like to make it fun." Tate dangled the handcuffs suggestively.

Jax sighed. So she was a walking nerve, and her body felt as if she would never get enough attention in all the right places. It was Halloween, and they'd both gone to a lot of trouble with their costumes. Why not get it over with so they could go out?

Her inner critic announced that a "get it over with" mindset was a guarantee that whatever they did, she'd be unsatisfied with the result. God, she hated these hormones.

She tried to improve her attitude. "Since when does Seven handcuff Janeway to anything? Janeway is the top."

Tate ran a hand over her foam-molded front. "Dream on!"

"She's the captain. By definition." Jax tossed her red hair for emphasis.

"Well, she can't be in control *all* the time."

"Pardon me, but a starship captain can be a top one hundred and fifty percent of the time. They have special training."

Tate, who'd already put on her Starfleet regulation boots,

reached for one of Jax's wrists. "Okay, consider this training. Just in case dear Captain Janeway should find herself captured by Seven-of-Nine clones with a bed-shaped tractor beam."

Various parts of Jax's body were delivering status reports. Clitoris: hard and aroused, Captain. Cunt: swollen and wet, Captain. Nipples: erect and playful, Captain. "I hate these hormones. I'm desperate to get laid, and the moment I ovulate it'll all stop."

"Why not make the best of them?" Tate put her arms around Jax's waist. Jax breathed in the scent of Tate's shampoo as she buried her face into the sleek blond hair. "C'mon, Jax. Let me handcuff you to the bed. It'll be wicked hot."

Jax closed her eyes. Tate was a darling, and a real sweetie. Every month she came up with something new and distracting so that Jax didn't feel quite so much like a bitch in heat. The idea *was* wicked hot, and if they didn't do something soon, she was going to soak through her Starfleet uniform.

Truthfully, if they didn't do something before they went to the party, she'd spend the whole night rubbing up against anything that moved and wanting to drag Tate back home to get handcuffed to the bed. So why not have the wicked hot sex first?

"Okay," she said weakly, knowing she sounded unwilling and ungracious. It was the hormones talking.

Tate positively scampered to the bathroom. In moments lube and towels were next to the bed. How predictable I am, Jax thought. She's so good to me. Tears threatened. She *hated* herself like this, and the closer to menopause she got the worse it was.

"Captain Janeway, I think you ought to get out of that uniform. I don't want you pulling rank on me."

"I just got it on."

"I can't do all the things I want with that one-piece Velcro unisuit in the way." Tate sidled up to her. "Can I help?"

Jax nodded as she turned her back. Tate ripped open the

Velcro, then kissed her way hungrily down Jax's back. She couldn't help a shiver.

"You're not the only one who gets hot as hell when you ovulate. I know what you're going to taste like and how much I'm going to enjoy it. I'm as wet as you are."

Jax would have said "I love you," but the lump in her throat was too big. She was so horny it felt unattractive and needy, but Tate knew just what to say.

Naked, she let Tate push her down on the bed. "I wonder how it would feel to come all over Seven-of-Nine's thigh."

"After the party, my dear captain. We can trash both costumes after the party. God, look at you."

Jax crossed her legs, but Tate pushed them apart again.

"Your cunt is so red and so wet. Jesus, I love it when you're this way."

"It's not like I have any control over it." Jax held back tears of frustration. Why was it so hard to ask Tate to take over and do everything?

"Yes, you do. Seriously," Tate added. "You could decide not to let me touch you. You could decide to toss me out and do yourself. I don't like either of those options, to tell you the truth." She settled on the bed between Jax's legs. "You could decide on a quickie and save the cuffs for later. You could decide to let me fuck you silly right now. Those are all choices within your control and the last two—I'm all for both of those."

"I know that with my head, but my body is making so much noise I can't believe it."

In her best Terminator voice Tate said, "I'll be back." Then she firmly kissed Jax's clit.

It felt as if thirty thousand volts had just shot through Jax's body. God. What was she waiting for? She spread herself on the bed and grasped the middle bar of the headboard. "Is this where you want me?"

"All the time."

"I'm so glad we went with wrought iron."

"Yeah, it's certainly been useful. Why don't you hold on right there and let me . . . climb . . . no wait—"

"Ouch! That's my arm." Jax scooted to one side.

"Sorry, honey. I didn't realize the chain was so short, yeah, your hands need to be right there. So, okay." Tate grinned down at her. "Give me one wrist."

Tate's crotch was only a few inches from her face and Jax lunged up to bury her face there. "Oh, you are wet, aren't you?"

"Stop that."

"Make me." Jax forced her hot breath through the fabric just to feel Tate shiver. She didn't struggle as Tate ratcheted a cuff around her left wrist.

"I don't want these to be too tight. I'll leave them a little loose even, okay? My dear captain, you must behave." Tate pushed Jax down to the bed again, then caught and held Jax's free hand. With a masterful bit of dexterity, she threaded the cuff around the thick middle bar and snicked it securely around Jax's other wrist.

The metal was as tight as scarves and ropes had ever been, with her arms tautly stretched over her head. Jax relaxed and took a deep breath. The cuffs slipped down her hands a little bit, but weren't so loose they would ever slip off on their own. She was bound until Tate released her. Tate had been right, it was wicked hot, and the pounding pulse between her legs was now not so much about hormones as it was about whatever Tate was going to do to her.

"Now you're mine," Tate whispered. "And you gave me such a good idea about what I want to do first."

Jax watched with rising heat as Tate stripped off her costume. True, being fucked by Seven-of-Nine was not exactly a tepid thought, and there were plenty of times that being naked while Tate was fully dressed was a total turn on, but tonight she wanted the friction of skin. "I'm glad you haven't glued on your Borg implants yet."

"You can still prepare to be assimilated." Tate leaned down to kiss her softly. "Enough of that, baby."

"I'm soaked, Tate." Jax hoped she didn't sound as whiney as she felt.

Tate straddled her midriff and looked down at her. "You do get me incredibly wet." She moved her knees further up the bed, then cupped Jax's face. Hunching forward, she held her puffed and slippery cunt just inches from Jax's mouth. "Eat me, baby, and make it good."

The cuffs were very confining, but Jax strained as high as she could. Tate lowered herself and they made delicious contact. Tate was soaked and hot and Jax loved the salty-sweet taste of her. She needed no urging to make it good, but that Tate was ostensibly giving Jax no choice about it further excited her. When Tate got into a raunchy mood there wasn't anything Jax wouldn't do for her, with her, to her.

"Ooo, your mouth is so good," Tate crooned. "Make me come."

Jax licked and sucked wetly at Tate's clit, following the familiar rise in her lover's voice. This was bliss, pure bliss, and her hormones had nothing to do with it. She loved doing this to Tate.

"Oh, Jax, Jax . . ." Tate shuddered above her and then grappled weakly for the steady iron of the headboard. "Oh, lord."

Jax enjoyed the sight of Tate all flushed and momentarily overcome. She shifted in place, trying to find a more comfortable position for her arms and was glad when Tate got off her chest.

Licking her lips, Jax asked, "Who just assimilated who?"

"Oh, you are just asking for it."

"Asking for what?"

Tate's gaze was both playful and desirous. "My strapping on an implant and giving you the fucking you deserve."

Jax couldn't help the way her legs spread farther apart. "I surrender, I surrender completely."

"Oh, yeah." Tate shinnied down Jax's body, dragging her nipples over Jax's stomach. "It's your turn to come."

Jax shifted again and even though she didn't want to stop Tate, her arms were abruptly too tight. "Honey, I'm sorry, but my thumbs are going numb."

"Oh? How weird."

"I think . . . this is totally hot, but they're really digging in. Maybe if they weren't around the headboard?"

Tate bent again to kiss Jax's clit. "I'll be back."

Tate rummaged in the bedside table drawer, then went into the bathroom. "Have you seen the key?"

"What key?" Alarmed, Jax added, "I didn't even know you had these until twenty minutes ago."

"I thought I put it in the drawer, but I don't see it."

"Oh *fuck*. Find the damn key, Tate." Trying not to curse further, Jax watched helplessly as Tate searched. Helplessness was not her best thing—sex was about the only time she'd even pretend.

"I'm so sorry. I put it in the drawer, I know I did." She emptied the contents of the drawer onto the floor. "There is no key here."

"Across the hall," Jax said desperately. "Jonny must have a key."

Tate gave her a hopeful glance. "You're right."

"God, I hope she's there."

Tate snatched up her robe. "Me too."

The apartment was very quiet while Tate was gone. Jax tried not to pull at the cuffs, but it was getting increasingly uncomfortable. How did anyone stand this for more than a few minutes? She couldn't feel her thumbs at all now.

The door opened again and Tate rushed over. "I got it, I got it."

Jax waited for blessed release, but it didn't happen.

"I don't got it," Tate said. She scurried out of the room again.

After another two minutes, Jax heard Tate returning. To her mortification, Jonny was with her.

"Hi, Jax." Jonny, her face framed by her spiky black hair, was openly grinning.

Jax knew she was vividly red. "It's not really funny."

"Yeah, it is. Later you'll think so."

Tate, about sixty seconds too late, covered Jax with her own robe.

"Aw, what'd you do that for?" Jonny peered at the cuffs, then pointed out something to Tate. "That's the double-lock. The tip of the key presses it down and then the cuffs won't keep tightening as you, um, play. But if you set it, you have to turn the keys both ways." There were two tiny clicks.

"Oh, thank you," Jax said. She managed to lower her aching arms. "God, that's so much better."

"Any ol' time," Jonny said. "I just love helping out damsels in distress."

Jax took note of the fact that Jonny was wearing only a robe as well. "Sorry we interrupted things for you. Make sure Aria gets some, uh, down time."

"Oh, she'll stay right where she is, and believe me, down time is what's on my mind," Jonny said over her shoulder. "I'd appreciate it if that's the only house call you'll need tonight."

Thanking Jonny profusely the whole while, Tate pushed her out the door.

Jax sat up, wiggling her tingling fingers.

"Honey, I'm so sorry. How are they?"

They both rubbed and soothed until Jax could feel her thumbs.

Tate wouldn't stop apologizing. "Let me make it up to you."

"How?"

"Name it."

Tears threatened again. Jax wanted to go to the party but now that she was no longer afraid her wrists would break off, her damn clit was throbbing again. "Can you just fuck me? Just *do* me?"

"Oh, hell, yes, baby. I thought you wouldn't let me touch you with a ten-foot pole after that."

"No poles. Just you. Please, Tate."

Tate swooped over her, pulling her close for a heated kiss. "Just me? Then I think I'm going to have to go deep, baby. Reach up from the inside of you to try and hold your heart."

Jax shoved Tate's hand between her legs. "God, yes."

"Lube, honey, let me lube up."

A half-sob escaped Jax. Normally, she'd offer to do that for Tate, but she was trembling so hard it was better to let Tate do it. All she could see was Tate. Everything else was a sea of red. Tate was spreading lube on the back of her hand, her wrist, then up her forearm. Then she gave Jax a look that could have set the bed on fire. "Get on your hands and knees."

Panting and dizzy, Jax quickly flipped over and stretched, cat-like. "This way?"

"Yes, like that. So I can look at your wet cunt while my hand slips inside."

The bed rocked as Tate moved behind her, and Jax shuddered as her cunt was slowly stroked. She was so unbelievably wet.

Tate's other hand began stroking her, too, then with deliberate slowness, two fingers slid into Jax's cunt. The pleasure of it was so intense that Jax nearly climaxed. Her eyes filled with tears. She gritted her teeth and tried to turn inside out so that Tate could touch everything.

She knew Tate had four fingers inside her from the pressure she felt. She loved the sensation and exhaled to relax completely. Tate groaned and Jax closed her eyes.

Fill me, she wanted to beg. Fill me, fuck me, just do it. Words wouldn't form. She shoved back against Tate just as Tate pushed forward and Tate was all the way in.

"Oh, Jax, that's so good. Your cunt feels so good."

In her mind she was begging, but only her hips seemed able to move. Tate pushed deeper, her hand twisting and curling until Jax felt the awesome fullness that she so often craved.

Tate pulled back slightly and Jax felt her flesh strain and stretch, then Tate went deep again. "I wish," Tate gasped, "I wish I could take your hand so you knew what this is like. It's so incredible, so un-fucking-believably incredible."

They began to rock and Jax felt the full range of Tate's motion, from the deep push that felt like it was opening her soul, to the pull of her wrist against the clasping muscles that would not let go. Something in the way Tate moved her hand brushed everything inside in just the right way. The center of her was being massaged, slow and hard.

"Turn over," Tate said softly. "Turn over while I stay inside you."

Yes, Jax thought. I want to see her face when I come. Tate helped her and Jax settled onto her back, but propped up on her elbows so she could watch Tate.

"See how deep I am? I could climb inside you tonight."

"Yes," was all she could manage. Tate began to fuck her harder and her head lolled back.

"Down, baby." Tate pressed on Jax's chest. "Lay back and hold your knees, hold your cunt open, let me fuck you."

The physical pleasure and intensity grew sharper, but emotion was rising too. The aching need to be taken this way was going to be satisfied, but not just by Tate's skilled and powerful hand. Tate's voice, aching with love and awe, was taking care of the other needs that her vulnerability always awakened. It wasn't enough to get fucked silly. She needed to be loved at the same time. She needed to know that Tate was enjoying the depths of her desire.

"You just got more wet. How do you do that? I love fucking

you this way. I love it when you're like this. I want to do it all to you."

Jax choked back a scream as Tate's tongue covered her clit. The release she so badly needed tightened her cunt and trapped Tate all the way inside her. Muscles she could not feel at any other moment clenched and unclenched and her clit jumped against Tate's tongue. She thrashed against the bed and only heard Tate's voice.

"You're beautiful, beautiful . . ."

Tears were the final release. Gathered close in Tate's arms, Jax cried into her shoulder. "I'll be okay in a minute."

"Take your time, honey. That was amazing. You were amazing."

In a few minutes, Jax knew she'd be pissed off that she felt better. "Thank you. For doing that."

"Oh, honey, thank *you*. That is such a gift, it's just so fantastic that I can do that to you and you like it so much."

Glad that the realities of her surging hormones were temporarily pushed aside, she fondly messed with Tate's hair. "Don't you be telling the crew."

"Not a word, Captain. You think I want any of them marking their calendars?"

"You mark your calendar?"

"Well, yeah." Tate looked at her as if she was slow. "I look forward to it, every month. We have great sex all the time, but days like today are the best. I get so wet and hot just thinking about how slippery and wet and sweet your cunt will be. I don't care that hormones are making it even better. When you get like that I've got my own *pon farr* going on."

"Oh." It helped that Tate actually liked her with a major case of cat scratch fever. Maybe she didn't hate those hormones quite so much after all. And being able to plan ahead for a fine time together—maybe Tate was onto something. "You're really good to me, you know?"

"Why wouldn't I be? You let me put out the fire, Captain." Tate kissed her. "I feel like I get a temporary promotion to Sex Goddess of the Known Galaxy."

Jax laughed. "We both need to shower again. We're going to be terribly late."

"We'll just explain that Janeway needed Seven to top her—"

Jax kissed Tate hard and fast. "Don't you dare. I'll demote you."

Tate's eyes were twinkling. "And to what rank, Captain?"

"Sex *Slave* of the Known Galaxy."

"And how, pray tell," Tate asked with another kiss, "is that a bad thing?"

Down Time

~3A~

"No," Aria said tersely into the phone. "I am not on call tonight. Richardson is on call. Find Richardson." She nodded at Jonny, who snapped the cell phone shut.

"Halloween is always busy," Jonny observed. "Burns, spontaneous tattooing without proper equipment and so forth."

"I'm sorry, honey. That should be the last one."

Jonny had just enough time to survey her handiwork before the phone chirped again. She flipped it open and held it to Aria's ear.

Aria took a deep, angry breath as she listened. "Why are you calling me? I just finished seventy-two, and I am *not* on call." She listened briefly, let loose with a string of Latin interspersed with words Jonny did get, like *saline* and *cold pack*. "Do that and find Richardson. I am *not* covering his shift. I need some down time."

Jonny clicked the phone shut again. She gave Aria a playful smile. "Just don't say you need some tied down time." She caressed the silk scarf that wrapped the wrist closest to her. "Let's make the world go away."

Aria closed her eyes. "Oh, please. I just want to escape it all. I love my work, but please take it all away tonight, Jonny."

"A massage, head to toe, and even these wonderful fingers of yours." Jonny leaned over to kiss Aria's full, sweet lips. "You'll get your own practice in time."

"Giving nips and tucks to suburbanites for large fees." Aria smiled, her eyes still closed. "So I can take all the restorative surgery for pediatric cases I want. Give me another five years."

Jonny pressed her fingers over Aria's lips. "That's enough shop talk. You're in my bed right now, and I am going to do whatever I want to you."

Aria's eyes opened. "Oh, Jonny, you have no idea how much I need you tonight."

"Yes, I do." Jonny slowly trailed her fingers down the middle of Aria's chest. "You're in control all the time. But right now, I'm in charge. You're not going to make any decisions from here on out."

"Jonny . . ."

"Yes?"

"I love saying your name, that's all."

"Say it all you like while I play with your body. You are, without a doubt, my favorite clay."

Aria shivered, then relaxed into a smile. "Jonny . . ." She settled into a steady breathing rhythm, and the lines of stress around her eyes and mouth finally eased.

Moving down the bed, Jonny finished tightening the last scarf that kept those long shapely legs apart. Spread-eagled, Aria was an artist's dream of sculpted lines and firm curves. She would start with those shapely, ebony calves, Jonny thought, and work her way up to Aria's lush thighs. Massage her for a long, long time, tell her everything she planned to do long before she even touched so much as a nipple. They had all night. Aria had proposed staying in or going out, and then said the magic words to Jonny: "You decide."

"No brainer," Jonny had said. "You need some down time."

She had just stretched out along Aria's left side when the

phone chirped again. Hiding a sigh, she checked the display, nodded ruefully at Aria, then opened it. She tried not to hold it too close to Aria's mouth.

"I don't care if Richardson is at his mother's funeral or a state dinner. He's had two days off, and it's his turn. I'm *not* on call. Tell him that I'll—oh fine, I'll tell him myself."

Jonny clicked for a new call, then found the speed dial entry for Richardson. Though she was tired of the interruptions, her inner imp was delighted that none of Aria's colleagues had any idea she was tied up while they talked.

Without any preamble at all, Aria said, "Don't make the nurses call me five times because you won't take your shift." She listened, rolling her eyes. "Like you're the only one who has plans tonight. If you don't take this shift I will make sure Sherbourne knows it, because I warned you last week it was the last time you pulled this stunt on me."

She shook her head the whole time she listened to the sputtering answer. "Where's the co-credit for the *Journal of Plastic Surgery* articles you promised me, huh? No, I'm done. I will not cover you again." Aria jerked her chin at the phone and Jonny disconnected the call.

"Call the hospital." Aria sighed while the call was connecting, then, after a polite greeting, said, "Well, I've told him it's his shift just now and if he refuses to take your calls then find Sherbourne wherever he is and let him know. Yeah, I know. He's going to chew my ass, too, but it's now Richardson's decision as to whether that happens or not."

Jonny let Aria take a few deep breaths, then said softly, "I'm going to turn this off for a while."

Aria nodded. "Fine. Please."

She cupped Aria's face and kissed her gently. "You're all mine now. And we're going to play all night."

"Jonny . . ." Aria breathed. "Melt me. Make me new again."

"Yes, sweetheart. That's exactly what I'm going to do."

Aria's left calf was half-done, fingers pressing out one knot after another, when a noise distracted her. Jonny tried to catch the source of it without disturbing Aria, whose breathing had gone steady and deep.

Someone was knocking at the door. Urgently.

She thought for a moment to ignore it, but it repeated a third time and she knew Aria was going to hear it sooner or later. "I'm sorry, baby. Somebody's at the door."

"Oh, shit. Why is it so hard to get tied down, massaged and laid?" Aria groaned and it wasn't the kind of groan Jonny really liked to hear.

"I'll be right back, and we'll start again. The night is still young." Grabbing up her robe, she wiped the massage oil off her hands as she hurried to the door.

A quick peek through the security glass revealed her neighbor, looking agitated. She wrapped her robe tight and opened the door.

"Tate, what's wrong?"

Tate was already bright red. "I was wondering if, um, do you have a handcuff key?"

Jonny blinked as she replayed what she thought Tate had just said. "A key. For handcuffs?"

"Yeah, I can't find ours."

"Gotcha. Stay right here." Jonny scrubbed her hands more on her robe, not wanting to get oil on her key ring.

Aria said wearily, "What is it?"

"Tate needs a handcuff key."

"Oh, you're kidding."

"Nope."

Aria snickered. "Wonder why she thought of you."

Jonny found the standard key on her ring and eased it off. "Be right back."

She didn't bother to hide her smile as she handed the key to Tate. "That ought to do it. Best of luck to ya."

Tate bolted back across the hallway and disappeared into her apartment. Who knew, Jonny thought.

"So where were we?"

"My gastrocnemius."

"And what a beautiful gastrocnemius it is too."

She had just gotten comfortable again when the urgent knocking on the door returned.

"Damnation!" Aria sounded as if she was going to cry.

"It's okay. I'll take care of it. She's probably just bringing the key back."

The moment Jonny opened the door Tate said, "I turned it, but they didn't unlock."

"Stay right here." Jonny hurried back to the bedroom. "I bet she set the double-lock. I won't be more than a minute, I promise." On impulse she leaned over to lick Aria's nipple, then blew on it.

Aria moaned as it stiffened.

"You stay right here and you think about me doing that until you lose your mind."

"Hurry, baby."

She followed Tate across the hall. Their apartment was a mirror image of her own. Tate led the way to the bedroom and she was treated to the sight of Jax stretched out on the bed. Jax was a natural redhead, oh yes she was. Aria owed her five bucks.

"Hi, Jax."

"It's not really funny."

"Yeah, it is. Later you'll think so." It was a shame when Tate tossed a robe over Jax. She and Aria had the same statuesque qualities. The image of them doing babe-a-licious things to each other was momentarily distracting.

She pointed at the tiny hole on the side, even though she was musing at how gorgeous Jax's red hair would look spread over Aria's cocoa thighs. It was just the artist in her, that was all. "That's the double-lock. The tip of the key presses it down and then the cuffs won't keep tightening as you, um, play. But if you set it, you have to turn the keys both ways." She demonstrated and the cuffs opened.

"Oh, thank you," Jax said. "God, that's so much better."

"Any ol' time. I just love helping out damsels in distress."

Tate practically pushed her out the door.

"Do anything, and I mean *anything*, she wants," was her parting advice. "I've still got a scar from the only time the key went missing with my girl."

She was nearly whistling when she went back to her own place. It was on the tip of her tongue to tell Aria about the whole thing when she realized Aria was weeping.

"Oh, baby, I'm so sorry." She scrambled onto the bed and slipped her arms around Aria's shoulders.

"Don't leave again, Jonny. Don't answer the phone, don't do anything but be here with me."

"You got it, sweetheart. I'm so sorry. Do you want me to untie you?"

"No," Aria said in a small voice. "You decide what to do."

"I know what I want to do to you." Jonny wiped the tears from Aria's face with the cuff of her robe. "I want this."

She hungrily kissed Aria's throat and felt a responsive shudder. The massage could wait. She shed the robe and covered Aria with her body, grinding their pelvises together. She kissed Aria until their panting prevented more. "I'm not going anywhere now. I'm going to enjoy you and nothing is going to stop me."

Inching downward, she moaned softly when she felt Aria's wet heat against her stomach. She moved her hand down, got her fingers wet, then painted the wonderful stuff onto Aria's nipples, gleaming light reflecting off her smooth, dark skin. "And I want this."

She rolled each nipple between her lips, licking them both clean in the process. Aria began to writhe and whimper as Jonny went back for more slippery stuff to smear on the rising tips. "You taste so good like this," she whispered.

She indulged herself for several more minutes, getting her fingers wet, then rubbing them over Aria's breasts. More and more turned on, she grasped one swollen point between her finger and thumb to lick at it greedily.

"Jonny . . . you're making me crazy, baby."

"That's the whole point."

Their pelvises rocked together again and Jonny wanted to feel Aria come underneath her. She slipped a hand down and started to play in the sleek, tight folds between Aria's legs. "You taste so good."

She watched Aria's eyes unfocus as she held her wet fingers up where Aria could watch Jonny lick them. She got them wet again, teasing Aria's clit, then rubbed them over Aria's mouth. Aria sucked eagerly at them and moaned when Jonny took them away.

"There's nothing but me loving you tonight. You don't have to think about anything but the way my fingers are touching you."

Aria strained up against the scarves as Jonny circled her clit. The noise she made was one of Jonny's favorites, so she circled it again, then gently squeezed the nub. Working Aria's body was like spreading paint with her fingers. Wild colors and soft textures, curving edges, all sculpted with a fingertip, or several, or her entire hand.

She knelt eagerly between Aria's legs, admiring the taut muscles and elegant lines. Then her gaze went to the short, kinked hair gracing Aria's pelvis and she ran her fingers over it, liking the texture. Aria brought out the artist in her like only paint and clay did. For her next birthday Aria had promised to let Jonny cast her gorgeous pussy in clay, and finish it in her own homage to Judy Chicago.

Homage was the right mood, and she bent to kiss Aria's pubic hair, enjoying the rough texture of it against her lips. If she lingered long enough—and she planned to—her cheeks would redden from the friction. Tomorrow someone might mention she looked a little sunburned. Given how hot Aria was, they'd be right.

Aria was breathing hard, but steady, with her eyes closed. Over the years Jonny had come to admire her ability to slip into a meditative trance that freed her normally stressed body to respond not just easily, but—with the right stimulation—massively. Tonight, there would be the right stimulation. No hospitals, no patients, no worries.

Jonny eased her tongue between Aria's lips, opening the tight curl of wet, inviting flesh. The deep red with the silken cream of Aria's excitement further darkened her hair and surrounding skin. She licked again, savoring the taste. Gorgeous.

She sank fully into loving this part of Aria with her lips, her nose, the full length of her tongue. Aria was her goddess and her muse. There was no limit to her worship, no rush to it either. She played, and played, and played. For a long, long time.

"Jonny . . ." Aria's tone was urgent, and Jonny shuddered out of her intense focus on Aria's taste and texture.

"Yes, sweetie, it's time." She licked her tongue firmly over Aria's clit as she slid two fingers inside her. "Time for you to come."

The ripples started immediately under her fingertips. Pulses of muscles and gushes of wetness caressed Jonny's hand while she flicked fast and hard at Aria's shuddering clit. First the adoration, then the sacred anointing, Jonny thought. She had always been and would always be a goddess worshipper.

Her face wet and smile pleased, she loosened the scarves binding Aria's ankles, then crawled up Aria's body to fully embrace her. "I'm never going to get enough of you tonight."

Aria was smiling, too, still breathless. "That's okay by me."

Jonny released Aria's arms, too, and they shared a long, shivering embrace. "Let's have some tea and start over. No phones, no neighbors, just you and me."

Cuddling on the sofa, warm mugs of tea in hand, Aria coaxed Jonny to talk about her progress on the work commissioned by the S.F. Arts Council. "Did you ever find the kind of stone you were looking for?"

"Just yesterday." Jonny smoothed Aria's shoulder as she talked. "It's a bright red and grinds easily, and it's got a lot of mica, so once I roll the clay in it, there's the light refraction I've been trying to get. If they do put it under the building overhang, it should stay reflective. But if not, the mica will dull from all the salts in the rain."

"Can they give you any assurance about the installation site?"

"I'm going to meet with the liaison next week. Meanwhile, I've got a couple of portraits to keep me busy."

Aria made a face. "You hate portraits."

"It pays my share of the rent, honey. I really don't mind." Jonny grinned at her. "I spend the whole time thinking about you."

The pleased blush that glowed in Aria's face was gratifying. Aria drained her tea and said, "How lovely it's a full moon for the festivities."

"I thought the outside lights were bright. Is that really the moon?" Jonny set her mug down and followed Aria to the window. With the blinds all the way up she could see that the moon had just cleared the building opposite them, the face glowing with reflected sunlight. Just like me after loving Aria, Jonny thought fancifully. "By golly, it is. Look at that."

"It's lovely."

She slid her gaze to Aria's upturned face, admiring the sharp line of light that etched her profile in silver. "Lovely."

Aria's lips twitched into a small grin. "You are so very good for my ego."

"Anything wrong with that?"

95

"No," Aria said softly. "I like it. And I like you." One hand drifted down Jonny's body, finding and stroking a nipple.

"Let's go back to bed."

"Nuh-uh." Aria pulled Jonny close for a possessive kiss. "You just lean against the windowsill, right there."

Aria's body was hot against the front of her while the glass was cold against her back. The contrast made Jonny's skin prickle in response to both extremes and her moan was easy as Aria held her face and kissed her. I'm the luckiest woman alive, she thought. She didn't think of the years she'd spent playing the field as wasted, not in the least. They'd given her the chance to appreciate what she had found when Aria had arrived in her life. To worship a goddess and have her worship in return—the artist in her loved the symmetry. And every time they joined she felt as if the work of art that was Aria continued to change and grow more beautiful, in part from Jonny's love.

Aria teased her legs apart and moved closer, continuing the long kisses and quiet, loving words. "I'm just going to love you right here. You just hold on, sweetheart, and enjoy the moonlight."

"Yes, ma'am." Jonny smiled into the next kiss and let the full impact of Aria's hand slipping between their bodies show in the shudder that swept down her body. Other women she might not have wanted to see how much she enjoyed simple caresses, but she'd always been an open book to Aria. The moonlight on her shoulders seemed to pour down her body to further heat Aria's hand, which moved with delicious, deliberate strokes.

She didn't understand compulsion or force, except that having a choice of how to experience pleasure mattered. For herself, an unabashed response to Aria's lovemaking was a choice. The easier the touch, the more awareness she had of her body's reactions. Aria's skilled fingers massaged her G-spot, then moved down to awaken all the nerves just inside her opening.

She put her head gently back against the glass, her legs going to jelly. Aria twisted her hand slightly and her thumb found Jonny's clit.

Her focus narrowed to the gleam in Aria's eyes and the insistent pleasure of Aria's hand. Any noise she might have heard was lost in the pounding of her heart. Every piece of art she'd ever created did not capture this kind of beauty. To her there was nothing more beautiful than the shared love of women.

The moonlight poured down her, and her climax seemed to join with it, washing her clean of worry and stress, purifying her for the few minutes when Aria held her tight and close.

"Let's go to bed," Aria whispered. "Sleep and then I think a little more down time for both of us."

"Shall I turn the phone back on?"

Aria grinned and gave Jonny a shy look. "You decide."

It was a no-brainer.

Up on the Rooftop

~Part 2~

Suze points at another cluster on the street. It's wild and crazy down there, and the binoculars give me a few close-ups of things I'd rather not have seen.

We're not alone on the roof anymore, but so far no one has challenged our right to be there. Apparently there's a party of some kind in the building and a number of people keep coming up for a while to watch the fun. The rooftop across the street is similarly lined with spectators gazing down at the fun in the street below us all.

Earlier, Suze dared me to go downstairs to the party for beer, and I finally did because I had to pee. The party was obviously for boys but there were enough girls there that I wasn't noticed. Suze was impressed when I reappeared with two cold ones. "I'm not the sweet innocent Midwest transplant you think I am," I had told her.

She hadn't answered but her eyes seemed to be saying plenty. I'm afraid to interpret it all. I feel such a fool. I'm dying for her to say *anything* that indicates she's romantically interested. Hell, I'd settle for a purely physical thing. At least for a while.

"Hey, let's move down here a bit. We won't be so much

behind those lights." Suze scoots our bags down the roof and the glare from the massive temporary lights reduces enough to clear my threatening headache.

"I thought there'd be more ghosts and goblins and Draculas."

"Too passé for the Castro."

I kind of miss such simple signs of Halloween. I am about to point out a topless woman (one of many) when motion in a window across from us catches my eye.

I focus the binoculars and see an older woman, her man-cut shirt unbuttoned, stepping back from the blinds. Probably most nights no one can see in, but the moon has risen and without the street glare I can see fairly well.

A much smaller woman, wearing a gorgeous Victoria's Secret special, complete with garters, steps into the older woman's arms, and they kiss. My head feels unbelievably hot all of a sudden, and for a moment I can't breathe. I fully expect the Victoria's Secret to be removed, but when they move to the bed—just barely visible—it is the other woman who ends up naked.

She is beautiful—maybe *handsome* is a better choice. The kind of handsome I hope I am in another twenty years. The smaller woman is on top of her and they move like they are on a waterbed, except they aren't. It's unbelievable. They ripple together, like they are made to do exactly that.

When the smaller woman moves down between the older woman's legs I feel faint. I want that, I want it so bad I can feel her breath on my bare skin.

"Whatcha watching?"

I drop the binoculars on my foot. "Just crowd stuff." I know I am blushing furiously.

"Oh, really?" Suze lifts her binoculars and peers at the apartment windows. "Oh. Oh! I see. Wow."

"Is that the woman in leather we saw earlier?"

"No, I don't think so. She was younger and definitely not that thin."

"This one looks like she bikes or runs or something."

"You're looking real close, aren't you?"

I'm still blushing. "So are you."

"Yeah, but I'm gay."

I put down the glasses. "Is there something you want to ask me, Suze?"

Suze keeps her binoculars at her eyes. "Are you gay, Amy?"

"Yes, Suze, I am."

We don't say anything for a while, which is good, because my stomach feels like someone just shoved it out through my throat.

Within a few minutes, Suze is pointing out a quartet of Veronica Lakes and an enormous wiener playing "Hail to the Chief." My stomach seems to have settled back into place.

The world has not come to an end.

I want in the worst way to look in the window but now that Suze knows I'd really like to, it seems incredibly awkward. I'd have to be officially dating someone to even begin to think about watching something like that at the same time. How do you get to the point of saying to anyone what does and doesn't turn you on? What if what turns you on grosses them out?

Nevertheless, when Suze heads down to crash the party for more beer and a pit stop, I train the glasses back on the window. The moon has moved slightly, so I can no longer see the whole bed. Just the smaller woman is visible, and she's naked now. Disappointed that she may have gone to sleep, I nearly stop peeping, but then she rolls onto her back. After a moment I can't see her face, and I realize it's because there's a leg in the way. Then it's a hip and I can hardly see the smaller woman because the tall one is completely on top of her.

I can barely swallow as I realize the woman on top is burying her face into the smaller woman's center and they are moving again with that rolling ripple like they were made to fit together exactly like that. *Sixty-nine* seems crude to describe it—it's so beautiful, so erotic I can't stop watching.

"God, that's hot."

Caught red-handed, I realize I was so engrossed in watching the two women that I didn't even hear Suze return and pick up her own binoculars. I somehow find my voice. "It's amazing. I didn't know two people could fit like that."

"That's not what I'm looking at," Suze says. "Go up a floor."

Reluctantly, I raise the glasses to the window directly above the one still framing the two deeply involved women.

The first thing I see, big as life, is the back of another woman, plastered against the window. She looks familiar. "Is that the leather woman we saw?"

"I'd say so," Suze says. "Wait a bit and you might get a glimpse of her girlfriend."

"Oh. Is that why she's . . ." The girlfriend comes into focus. She's dark and gorgeous. They're all gorgeous. Women are gorgeous and I'll never think otherwise. For a moment, they are turned toward each other with a smile, and I can see both profiles until they merge into a slow kiss. Then the leather woman's head rests back on the glass and her mouth is open. I want to hear the sounds she must be making. I wish I were a mouse on the wall. I wish I lived in that building, that's for sure.

I retrain the glasses on the floor below. The two lovers have moved apart and, dang, it looks like they're going to sleep. Shoot.

"Well that's worth standing up here in the cold for hours," Suze says. Her voice sounds a little bit tight, like maybe she's having as hard a time breathing as I am.

If I close my eyes I can see Suze and me on a bed, enjoying each other at the same time. I can see me framed in the window while Suze touches me in whatever way lesbians touch. I think I know but until one touches me, how can I be sure? Whatever it is, it'll feel fantastic.

"Don't you think so?" Suze has turned to me and I realize I've got to say something.

"Yeah, it's worth it."

She gazes at me for a long, long time and I can't breathe and I don't think she is breathing either, and I really don't want to go back to watching the crowd. I want to go someplace and be alone with Suze and let whatever happens just happen.

I can't tell if it will be hard to convince Suze to do that. Part of me wants it to be easy and the rest of me is terrified it will be. I'm not ready for lesbian sex, says the terrified part. The rest of me is so ready that my neck is sweating.

Suze finally says, "Are you ready to call it a night?"

Yes. No. I don't know. Maybe.

I've come so far, so fast. I want to jump out of the plane, sure, but I don't even know what a lesbian parachute looks like. I want to trust Suze, and let her guide me all the way to the ground, but it's scary. And I don't know why I'm thinking about planes and parachutes when she's looking at me, expecting me to answer.

I have no idea what to say that's got anything to do with who I want to be, who she is, and whether there are life forms on other planets and if so, are they lesbian? How can such a simple question be so hard to answer? It's not as if she's asking me to go to bed with her.

Or maybe she is. Why can't I be Melissa Etheridge's love child, growing up knowing what I want from the beginning instead of stumbling around thinking nonsense when the woman I really, really, really want to kiss me looks at me as if I've lost my mind?

I bend over my scattered belongings, hoping to find bits of my brains.

Tick, Tock

~2D~

Sometimes, life with you can slip inside an instant and play out after tick but before tock. And I am suspended.

A thousand moments with you shape my thoughts. You are always at the window, sometimes your face crimsoned by sunrise. I'd watch you every morning for the rest of my life if I could. You know I would. I want to live in this instant for years, when you're aware that I am standing here, loving you, and you've not yet turned to greet my morning kiss. That you love me is the miracle of my life.

Tonight, as every night, you are cast in silver moonlight. I'd want to live in this instant too. The cold breeze from the window lifts the white curtains, which dance and swirl with your long, pale gown. I'd watch the rise of night in the glow of your eyes and know, when you look at me, that I am made whole.

I didn't know what complete was until your touch. Other lovers were good to me, but you were the missing piece of my life.

Do you remember when we met? I thought you were cold and you thought I was stuck up. It makes me laugh, recalling how we sniped at each other all through that double date. Our friends finally gave us leave to go, remember? We walked out of the restaurant at the same time and stood talking next to your car for two hours.

When you finally said yes and admitted you liked it when I begged, we stayed in bed for two whole days. Remember when you came back from the kitchen with the hand mixer and said you'd heard it was the latest in sex toys? I nearly believed you and called you my kind of pervert.

I'm so glad that we called in sick that day in the spring and drove up the coast to the Headlands. The beach was long and deserted, and we sat in the sun while the wind tried to tear the coats off our backs. We stood gazing, later, at the brilliance of the Golden Gate as if we'd never seen it before. I felt new. We kissed shyly. The beauty of the day was only more so for your eyes gazing at me.

We stopped at that deli and got sandwiches and ate them in the car with the ocean crashing only feet away. The sharp wind was too chilly for either of us to bear for long, but an hour with you in the car was all the happiness of a lifetime.

I think about that trip all the time. Remember the bed-and-breakfast we stayed at when we headed on up to Bodega Bay? How we were pretty certain that nobody at breakfast would look at us because of the noise we'd made the previous night? I still say we weren't that noisy, but it's always been true that when you come, most of the neighbors know.

I know, yes, there was that woman who complained before we moved here, then called the cops. How funny that one of them was a dyke, and when we explained you were trying to become a professional yodeler she wanted so bad to laugh. You showed your badge, said it wouldn't happen again and that was that. A few months later we moved anyway. Nobody in this building has ever complained and more often than not we heard them at night. You're right, I think. There's something in the water.

I remember everything we ever did in bed. The taste of you,

the texture of the small of your back, the way your eyes change color when you want me the most—I think about those things all the time. Your lovely blue eyes go purple as we make love and we laugh.

That night, in the B and B, if the other guests heard anything, it was us laughing. What I like about laughter is you can do it in public and it feels good. I remember a thousand shared laughs with you. I can hear them all in my head. I could live happily in any of those moments and never want another thing.

On the way home, the next day, I remember we went wine tasting, and you got tipsy. So adorable, and you giggled so infectiously other people couldn't help themselves. You made me pull over on that back road, remember? Under the tree? You said it would be quick so we got in the back seat. But you were tipsy so you couldn't quite come, and we were there for nearly an hour, ducking down when cars passed, which only made you giggle more.

Eventually you sobered and made me get off the freeway on the drive home. Quick, hard, fast, behind a ubiquitous gas station. You came, we switched places, and I did too, and we both spent the rest of the drive with sodden pants.

I wish I could remember what exit we'd taken for that gas station. I've driven it, trying to remember, but no place seems right. It was such a good time, and I'd like to be clear. Take a picture of the place and add it to the scrapbook of Us.

Tonight, I want to stay between *tick* and *tock*. Look at you in the moonlight, where you are so real these days. The light shimmers at the window, and I swear there is a mist that could be your face. You are there, waiting. I feel you, guarding me, keeping me safe—even from me. You protected the weak, rescued the defenseless, stared down the boogeymen. Sometimes I look at the bottle of sedatives the doctor prescribed and yet I never take more than one because you are there in the moonlight, the sunrise, in my every thought.

Am I crazy that I think that cat burglar gave up on this building because you are guarding it, keeping watch from our window? That even on a night like tonight, with the raucous crowd outside in the street, nothing evil will happen nearby? You won't allow it. You keep me safe, the way you always have. You wanted to keep the world safe. I've made myself forget the name of the little girl who is alive because you're not. I can't think about that right now. I can only think about you, wrapped in moments when we were happy.

I remember every minute. I remember every laugh, every word, every tiff and every make-up kiss.

But I can't remember the damned gas station where we made love for the last time. It's driving me crazy, honey. I wish you could help me remember.

I wish you could help me. I know you'd hate me this way, but I don't want to move. I don't want to go anywhere. I don't want to eat or sleep. Wrap me in cold arms and lavish me with vapor kisses. I don't care as long as it's you, and it *is* you, no matter how crazy that sounds.

I just want to remember you, at sunset, at sunrise, in the moonlight. I want to remember you any way I can, except the last way I saw you, going out the door to another night of patrol.

You're not a statistic, you're the woman I love. I remember everything so vividly that you're real, and standing right there, at the window. You're turning now, because you know I'm here.

Look at me.

I love you. I won't stop.

You can come back. Please.

If I sleep you'll go away. So I won't sleep tonight, and we'll be together. We can stay here between *tick* and *tock*, forever.

Nine-Inch Nails

~3D~

"Pete! Order up for Pete!"

With a start I realized the barista was calling for me, and I hastily secured my hot chocolate.

"Trick or treat?"

"Huh? Oh." I stuck my hand into the bag the barista held out and came up with a chocolate kiss. Now it felt like Halloween to me. "Thanks."

I had nearly scored a seat in the crowded café, but the arrival of a large party of gangsters and floozies took the last of the chairs. So I leaned against the plate glass window and watched the parade of Castro humanity while my cocoa cooled and the kiss melted in my mouth. My camera battery was already dead and though home was just up the street, I didn't want to miss anything.

Not that I have anything against any of my Sapphic sisters, but after the fifth Xena and Gabrielle combo I was noticing the guys a lot more. Originality, wit, style and legs to die for—men in the Castro can be the most delicious looking females on the planet.

Diana Ross and the Supremes, the secretary of state, flaky

first daughters, Ethel Merman and Sweet Potato Queens—it was all here in the Castro. I enjoyed the show, though I quickly remembered to keep my gaze above the waist. Hairy male butt was not high on my list, even if it was one of the most innocent sights of the evening.

I was about finished with my hot chocolate when there was an outburst behind me. So much for my belief that dykes were more sedate. One of the gangsters leapt to her feet, shouted, "Butch cock! Whatever happened to butch pussy?" and ran out. A floozy took off after her, moving fast in spite of killer stilettos, and I shared an amused glance with a totally hot female all decked out in biking leather. The outfit was probably borrowed, but who the hell cared? She was divine to watch walk away. Keri had walked like that, once upon a time.

The music changed from some slow soulful piece to a hard, industrial grind. Half the tables cleared in the first minute, which probably was the intent of the music change. As I was tossing away my empty cup I saw at least a dozen cloaked figures pass the doorway, all of them shrouded in black from head to toe except for prominent green dildos strapped just where you'd expect them to be, bouncing heavily as the group marched along.

I guess my jaw dropped a bit because the woman with the multiple piercings, who'd been glancing through the weekly paper, said, "Something wrong?"

"What in hell is that?"

"Nine-inch nails."

I blinked. "Okay. Why green?"

It was her turn to blink. "Head like a hole."

I was still trying to figure out how to intelligently respond to what she'd said when she waved a hand at the open air.

"Nine Inch Nails—this song is 'Head Like a Hole'." She didn't add, "Are you deaf or something?" but she certainly was looking like she wanted to.

"Oh!" I grinned. "I thought you were talking about the dozen green dildos that just marched by."

"Oh hell, did I miss the Satanic Leprechauns?"

She was gone before I could say another word.

There's nothing like the Castro on Halloween, really.

The night air was sharp and cool, and the street was thick with revelers. Catcalls, cheers, music—it was one long, boisterous cacophony. The windows of most of the surrounding buildings were filled with spectators, some of whom threw Mardi Gras beads. I flashed and scored a slew of purple even though I was just in jeans and a black tee. They were all girlie-girls, and my extra short hair and lack of bra was apparently to their liking.

I caught sight of the Satanic Leprechauns again, as well as the gangster who'd fled the café. She was occupied in a doorway in deep conversation with the floozy who'd followed her out the door.

It must have been ten p.m., because speakers blasting out of the bars changed over to the radio station that was doing a rock-and-roll Halloween party hosted by a prominent gay comic. After some patter, the whole street began rocking to "Let's Get it Started in Here," and the serious dancing and posturing began.

I wandered for another hour, joining in with some group body-bouncing a couple of times, then I headed for home. Even in the lobby I could hear the party in 1A at full blast. I couldn't pass the second floor without thinking about the poor women in 2D. One of them had died in the line of duty last year—what a shock that had been. As I reached the third floor I thought maybe I'd get Keri and bring her down, but it would depend on how she was feeling.

"Hey, honey. How's the crowd tonight?" Keri turned her head as I entered, looking relaxed and pleased to see me.

"Wild and crazy." I related the tale of the green dildos as I booted up the computer. "Ready for a picture show?"

"Sure." Keri nudged her chair closer to the desk, and I tipped the screen so we could both see it.

"Hungry? Can I get you anything?"

She hefted the mug resting in the cup holder I'd bolted to the front of the chair's left armrest. "I'm fine. Oh—don't do it tonight, please. But I think the belt's slipping on this thing again."

"That stuttering noise?"

"Yeah."

"I'll pull the motor apart tomorrow. Here we go—I caught the second set of the individual costume contest."

We clicked through the couple hundred photos on the camera's memory chip and I narrated so that Keri could have more of a feeling of having experienced it herself. She hadn't felt comfortable in a Halloween crowd since going from a walker to the chair, and my photos were the lifeline to our neighborhood.

"So you didn't get a picture of the Satanic Leprechauns?"

"No—battery was dead. It was creepy."

"It's Halloween. Besides, how creepy can green dildos really be?"

I'm as bawdy as the next girl, I suppose, but the military marching and fully enveloping cloaks had been a little too *noir* for my tastes. "I like the Great Pumpkin, and Snoopy and bobbing for apples. People were dancing for the love of it, but there was also some heavy pick-up action going on. I love the Castro at Halloween, but . . . it could be fun without the dark sex overtones too."

Keri shrugged. Before MS she'd been the kind of witch top who had a little something extra under her skirt for me to appreciate. I'd never forget that night, it was true. Dark sex overtones had been her specialty, many nights throughout the year. "You

118

are right—Nine Inch Nails sounds like something we could buy at Good Vibrations."

"They looked like nine-inchers, that's for sure." I smiled at the memory of the bobbing dance they'd done. Attached to showgirls or stomping dyke daddies, I'd have found them far more amusing.

"I was thinking," Keri said softly, "that it's time to go shopping."

My hands stilled on the keyboard. "We can't go over to the Valencia store tonight."

Keri's voice, low and sexy, made my ears turn red. "There's always online."

"What brought this on?"

"You. You've got beads—so my woman was out there showing herself to other women. I think I need to remind her who she's with. Besides"—a little purr of laughter softened her voice even further—"you wouldn't believe the things I've heard through the walls tonight. There was major headboard action next door for at least an hour."

I glanced at her expression, and my body immediately responded to the eager, heated glint in her eyes. It had been true from the day we'd met—whenever, however she wanted me, she had me.

My breath felt tight in my chest as I clicked over to the Good Vibes Web site.

"Let's see what's new," Keri suggested as she put her hand on my bare arm.

I was intensely aware of the warmth of her touch as I navigated the pages. "Oh, look," I said with mock cheerfulness. "They've got a new dolphin vibrator."

Keri chortled. "With an interestingly placed dorsal fin. I know why some women prefer non-representational toys, but really, that just makes me think of Flipper."

"I don't want a dolphin doing me, thank you."

"Not to mention that when I do you, I don't want anything faster than lightning." She trailed her fingertips on my forearm, and I was once again aware of the heat of her hand. "Now what," she asked with a philosophical tone, "do you suppose you do with that little bunny?"

"No rabbits," I said firmly. "No little Bunny Foo Foo for me."

Her fingernails grazed my skin. "Well, we'll just have to find something you do want. Go to the silicon page."

A few clicks later she squeezed my arm, and I paused scrolling. "Which one?"

"The green one, of course. Was that what the leprechauns were wearing?"

"No, too short."

"Look at the ridge, that's fairly pronounced. I think your G-spot would like that." Her fingers traveled up my arm to my shoulder, then down again, raising goose bumps in their wake.

My pants were feeling too tight now. "My G-spot likes everything you've ever used."

"Take your clothes off," she said softly. It was not a request.

Lost in her deep brown eyes, I stripped without much ceremony. Once upon a time, Keri had taken twenty minutes just removing her blouse, driving me into a frenzy.

When I was naked, she said, "Very nice. Kiss me."

I straddled the chair in her favorite position for me—one foot on the ground and my opposite knee between her thighs. I was completely exposed to her, which we both liked.

She cupped the back of my head with her still powerful left arm and pulled me to her. Her mouth tasted of peppermint tea and she bit my lower lip when she broke the kiss. "I can smell you. Wet for me, aren't you?"

I nodded. "I'm always wet when you want me."

"Good." Her smile was edged with that dangerous intensity

that had caught me from the very start. "Do you like the look of that green toy?"

One finger flicked my clit and I gasped. "Yes."

"I confess, I'd love to watch you playing with it. Too bad it's not here."

"Maybe," I stopped to swallow hard as her finger and thumb caught and tugged gently on my swollen clit. "Maybe we can use something we've already got."

"We'll just have to make do, won't we?"

I gathered her long, dark hair in my hands. "Whatever you want."

"Let's go to bed."

I traced the delicate arch of her eyebrows with my thumbs, then softly, slowly, kissed her again. The physical therapist had predicted that Keri's libido would wane as the MS progressed. I believe her fierce conviction that sex starts in the brain had kept Keri acutely interested in one of the few things she could still do with ease—turn us both on.

When once we might have said "you get the towels" and "I'll get some water" on our way to bed, the last few years the dialogue had changed. But the intent was the same—we never went to bed without first making sure we were both comfortable. As she pulled herself from the chair to the bed I asked where her numbness was sharpest tonight. Listening to her answer, I fetched the right pillows. She asked if I was cold tonight while she pulled back the rest of the bedclothes.

Just as Keri had found a position she preferred for me over her wheelchair, she likewise had decided just how she wanted me arranged in bed. Her command of the setting was nothing new. From the very first she had been very particular about everything in the bedroom and I had loved it then. I loved it now.

Propped up on pillows behind her back and shoulders, she cradled my shoulders and head in her lap. I automatically opened my legs and lifted my knees slightly.

"That's right," she said quietly. "Be open and ready for me."

My breath was already short and my pulse pounding, and those sensations intensified as she handed me the blindfold. I slipped it into place, without hesitation, and let my world narrow to the feel of Keri's hand on my body and the sound of her voice.

"I think we'll need this," she mused conversationally as she moved some items from the drawer at her side to the towel next to me. "And this, and a lot of this."

I wondered what Keri was selecting for me. I knew she'd set them down on her right side, where both of us would be able to reach them. "We won't need much lube."

The dark silk of her voice seemed to pour over my ears. "By the time I'm done with you, we will. Show me." Fingers squeezed my nipple, rolling it so firmly I squirmed. "Show me how you put lube on when you want me to fuck you."

I grappled for the bottle and squeezed slippery, cool lotion onto my palm.

"Touch yourself," she commanded softly. "I want to watch you."

I held back a whimper as my slick fingers moistened my already wet folds. The blindfold allowed me to focus on sensation and to let memories and fantasies wash through my mind. Every image of intimacy with Keri was reinforced by the deliberate impact of her voice on my thoughts.

"Open yourself, let me see your clit. One finger, right on top, that's right . . . slow. Light, slow. You're trembling in anticipation, aren't you?"

My skin was tightening on my bones. My nipples felt like rocks as she casually tweaked and pulled them. "Yes, Keri, I'm ready. You know how I get."

"Oh yes, I do know." Her hand drifted over my body, smoothing my stomach and circling my belly button. "You'd like one of those big green dildos right now, wouldn't you?"

122

My clit was swelling under my fingertip. "I want whatever you choose for me. That's all I've ever wanted."

"So if I told you to stop and we'll just go to sleep, you'd be fine with that?"

A whimper escaped. "Please don't stop."

"Are you wet now?"

"Yes, very."

"Then I want you to pick up the toy I've chosen for you."

I fumbled on the bed next to me, and found the smooth solidity of a dildo. I knew it right away and half-smiled. Keri had an appetite tonight. After looking at sex toys with her online, I did too. That was part of the reassurance of knowing each other so well.

"More lube on your hands, and show me how wet you need to be." Keri was again pulling on my nipples while her voice grew huskier. "Get that nice big toy wet enough to go inside you."

Another squeeze from the bottle had everything as slippery as I could need. "I'm ready," I said softly.

"Relax," she whispered. With her weaker right hand, she stroked my scrub-brush short hair. "I want this to be good for both of us. I love fucking you."

She pinched my nipple as she spoke and I arched up, my knees falling even more open. I was anchored to her by her voice and her hands.

"Touch your clit with the head of my cock."

I groaned at the contact, falling deeper and deeper into the well of our mutual lust. When the therapist had suggested we might need to find other ways to enjoy sex than direct touch, we had both smothered laughs. From the earliest days we'd played on the phone, or as we did now, with me responding to Keri's suggestions. Her knowledge of how I liked to be touched, the rise and fall of arousal in her voice and the way she pushed my erotic buttons were everything I could ask for in a lover.

"Oh, you sound so wet, baby. Slide the head of my cock between your lips. Up . . . and down . . . oh yes, just like that. Tease your opening."

My hands were an extension of her now, and I thrust my hips up, hungry for penetration, even as I kept the promise of it at the tease Keri wanted.

"You want it, don't you?"

"God, yes."

"Slip inside—just a little."

With a throaty moan, I eagerly pushed in. It felt so good.

A sharp tug on my nipple stayed my hand. "That's enough for now. Tease your cunt. In . . . and out. All the way out."

"Oh, please. God."

"Are you listening, Pete?"

"Yes." I was panting, the head of the toy just inside my lips.

Her voice was low and heated. "Now . . . shove it in. All the way in."

Parted, opened, taken, oh fuck, I thought. I loved the way she took me, all at once. Her hand was squeezing my breast and I could hear her labored breathing.

"That's right. Fuck yourself. Show me, show me how good it feels."

"Yes," I said through gritted teeth. "It feels so fucking good."

"Harder." She growled, throaty and low. "Open your legs and take it. Harder!"

"God, Keri, yes. Fuck me!"

"Do you remember the first Halloween when we were dating? When I did you in the alley behind the reviewing stand? You never knew you were waiting for a femme to rock your world instead of the other way around, did you?"

The memory of that night, the night I'd let go of what everyone else said was how a butch ought to be, played over my skin like a flash fire. Keri had pushed me against the wall, pulled up her witch's gown and pushed her cock between my thighs while her hand went down my pants. That night she'd slipped inside my head forever.

"Deeper. Take it all. Shove down on it."

The fullness of her cock pushed aside muscle and massaged open nerves. I felt an early gush of climax and thrust up with my hips, drawing out my response.

"That's right. Not yet." Keri's thighs stiffened, and I worried I was hurting her, then I heard the low hum of her vibrator.

The realization that she was going to come too sent me over the edge. I plunged the toy as deep as it would go, and my body stiffened as I soaked the toy.

"Oh, yes, baby, I can hear you coming, keep coming, baby, I'm almost there."

My body was dissolving with pleasure, melting into her lap and the bed. I moved the toy just a little so she could hear how wet I was. "We had to come home because I soaked my pants, your legs, your shoes, and did it again when you kept on fucking me."

"I didn't know you could do that. God, the way you come. Oh, Pete," she breathed. Her legs rippled with the onslaught of her climax and her entire body heaved upward once before she collapsed against the pillows.

I wanted in the worst way to take off the blindfold and rearrange us so we could spoon and cuddle. But I had to wait for her permission, not because she cared about the blindfold once I'd climaxed, but she did care about me seeing her before she'd fully recovered.

As I waited I admitted to myself, because honesty is one of the things that has helped us both through her diagnosis and treatment, that while I wore the blindfold I could imagine her the way she had been, and for that little space of time, it was what I needed. I acknowledged my anger and helplessness at her illness, and then put them away because in the light of her eyes they had no use.

"Hey," she said softly.

I took off the blindfold and blinked up at her. "I love you."

Her smile was soft and unguarded. "What is it about Halloween in the Castro? I've been hornier than hell all day."

"I don't know. I love the sex, don't get me wrong. But sometimes I'd like to be six again."

We shifted around so I could spoon her against me. Once the covers were settled around us she reached for the remote control.

"Happy Halloween," she said as she pressed the buttons.

"Wasn't that gift enough?"

"Oh, I'd do that to you any day of the year."

Familiar, beloved piano music began and suddenly I wanted to cry. Linus explained his philosophy of Halloween to Charlie Brown's sister. "Thank you, sweetie. It's a cure for Satanic Leprechauns."

"I thought you'd like it."

After a few minutes, she fell asleep and I watched the rest of the program. After I turned off the TV I realized how noisy the streets outside still were. From the window I could see one corner of Castro Street. Rows of Dorothys in ruby slippers danced until they were out of my sight.

Avast!

~3C~

"That looks absolutely stunning."

Renee temporarily turned her gaze from her own reflection to Jane's. "You don't look so bad yourself."

She watched Jane sidle up behind her and didn't bother to hide her shiver as Jane's lips nuzzled the nape of her neck.

"I think the shoulders should be like this."

Renee couldn't help but blush as Jane untied one more of the ribbon lacings on the front of her chemise. "I'm already barely covered."

Jane pulled down the short linen sleeves of Renee's costume, baring her shoulders. "I know, and I love it. And thank you for the hair—I know it took forever."

She put a slightly shaking hand to what could only be called a mane. Curls and ringlets surrounded her face and brushed the tops of her shoulders, while the rest cascaded down her back. "I thought it would enhance the whole wenchish look."

"It does," Jane breathed. Her hands swept around Renee's front to weigh each breast. "I love you without a bra."

Renee clutched the counter as her lover's firm body pressed against her. Jane groaned, and they were abruptly moving together. With a shudder, Renee admitted, "I'm so turned on that if you don't stop . . ."

Jane stepped back. "None of that. Later, sweetheart. Let me look at you."

After a slow pirouette, Renee leaned back against the counter to take in all of Jane's costume. She was aware that her bare legs were silken and alluring, and that Jane was mightily distracted by the sight of them against the casually ripped fine linen skirt. She shifted her weight to move the highest tear along her inner thigh.

"What pirate wouldn't want to ravage you, looking like that?" Jane hooked her thumbs in her wide leather sash with a possessive leer.

Renee took the one step necessary to lift her lover's hands from the belt. Smiling, she surveyed Jane's costume. "You look marvelous in breeches. And that shirt, all that muslin."

"Arrr!" Jane wiggled her hips. "It's not me breeches you'll be wantin', lass, but what's under 'em!"

"Oh, no hokey accents."

"Avast! What yonder wench stiffens me resolve?"

"I've never heard it called a resolve before," Renee quipped. Torn between laughter and wanting to wrap her hand around what she knew Jane had on under the breeches, she turned back to the mirror, uncharacteristically flustered.

Jane was behind her again, with another of those soft, loving kisses on the nape of her neck. "Are you sure, sweetheart? We don't have to go through with it."

Meeting Jane's gaze in the mirror, Renee said firmly, "I am absolutely sure. I've always wanted to do this."

"So have I. But . . . it really is up to you."

"I know." She fumbled with the powder puff, dusting her breasts lightly. "That head scarf is quite rakish."

"Wait until you see my tricorn hat." Jane nudged Renee's bare feet with the tips of her shoes. "Like the boots?"

Renee swallowed hard. "Very much."

Moving even closer, Jane whispered, "Did you know that *avast* means *stop*, but also *hold fast*?"

Renee shuddered as Jane's hands circled her wrists. "No, I didn't. Do we need to get out the pirate dictionary?"

Jane's hips moved against Renee. "Oh, I've already read through it. Do you want to? Or are you stalling, sweetie? Really—"

"I mean it, Jane. I do want to. So much my thighs are wet."

Jane's little gasp was followed by a heartfelt, "God, I want you."

"Then let's go."

Holding hands they walked to the door. Before Jane opened it, she took Renee into her arms. "I love you. And cherish you. All you will ever have to say is *stop*."

Renee rubbed her lips softly against Jane's. "Yes. That's my word for the night, darling. *Yes*."

A shiver ran through Jane's body, and the kiss they shared left Renee breathless.

Jane slowly turned the knob and opened the door with one last question in her eyes. Renee nodded as Jane caressed her bare shoulder, then wound her fingers in the thick waves and curls on the back of Renee's head.

Another nod, and Jane shoved Renee through the doorway.

The wench caught herself on the wrought iron frame of the captain's bed. She let her fear show as she turned to her captor. "Please let me go."

"If I do that," the steely-eyed pirate answered, "you end up prize for the whole crew. You are my prize alone. I would not share such as you." She felt a lustful grimace steal over her face as she admired the heaving bosom and long, smooth legs. "I apologize for the rough handling by the crew. I assure you, I can be far more gentle."

131

The wench lunged for the door but was easily caught once more by the strong arms. Kicking and struggling, she pleaded again, only to be lifted off her feet and dumped unceremoniously onto the bed. She rolled to one side, but the pirate pinned her face down.

"Let's not waste all our strength on fighting, sweetheart. I intend to have you, but would prefer you be more still." From the deep pocket of her breeches she pulled a leather thong and quickly bound the lovely wench's wrists. She would coax the fire out of this beauty. Her cabin had been too long empty and her bed too long cold.

The woman under her stilled, finally. "I cannot fight you."

"We can do far more pleasant things, sweetheart." The pirate rolled the wench over and could not hold back an earthy groan. The dim light of the sputtering lamp illuminated one full rose-tipped breast, exposed by their struggles. The torn skirting had slipped aside to leave the firm legs bare. "You are beautiful and desirable."

"You could never please me as a man would," the wench pronounced.

"Oh, sweetheart, I have no intention of pleasing you as a man would." One hand drifted over the trembling body, going near all the places the pirate wished to kiss and suckle, but touching none, not yet.

"The tie is hurting my wrists."

"Let me take care of that." From under the bed she drew a length of soft, white rope. Straddling the wench's waist, she wound the rope around the bed's iron frame and brought two slip-knotted loops to rest above the wench's head. "This will be far more comfortable."

In spite of her struggles and proud words, the wench could not help the shiver that seemed to crackle over her body. No man had ever pleased her. No man had ever known how to master her. "Comfortable for whom?"

The pirate leaned down, knowing that the pressure of the leather thong on the wench's bound wrists must be uncomfortable with her hands trapped underneath her. "For both of us, sweetheart. You will be able to pull, twist, struggle all you like, but you will still be mine. Do not lie to me that you are not excited at that prospect."

"Never!"

"I can smell you," the pirate whispered. "The hunger between your legs is increasing with every moment."

The wench's jaw slackened just enough for the pirate to know she was reading this fire cat correctly. From the moment their paths crossed, the fiery, defiant gaze had not masked the deep desire. "Take what you want, then! You'll still give me nothing I need."

The pirate rose to her knees and drew her knife from the sheath at her hip. "Roll over, my girl, and I'll free you. For the moment."

The wench eyed the knife nervously, the fear in the pit of her stomach threatening to rise up. She wriggled onto her front, aware that her chemise had slipped even further down her shoulders. With a shudder, she realized she could deny the pirate nothing. There was no place in her the pirate would not take, and no place in her that she did not want taken.

She broke out in goose flesh at the touch of the cold steel against her hands. She had thought she might try to resist further, but the awareness of the knife kept her still.

"Roll over again, my sweet."

She obeyed, carefully, and quickly saw that the knife was once again in its sheath. She began to raise her arms to push the pirate off of her, but the pirate easily caught both and stretched out on top of her.

"Resist me if you feel you must, but I shall have what I want right now. This . . ."

A wave of weakness blossomed in the wench's heart at the

tender touch of the pirate's mouth to her own. The wave gave way to a pleasure so deep she felt it in the soles of her feet, in her sex, in the rising tautness of her nipples.

Too late she felt the pirate lifting her arms to the waiting loops of rope. Her opportunity to struggle would be gone once they were tightened, but she moved too slowly. In moments her arms were stretched above her head.

"I will never surrender."

The pirate lifted herself off the wench's body. "I've not asked for the white flag from you." With a low growl, she stooped to catch one nipple between her teeth. The wench's body came up off the bed, and she smiled fiercely. "I don't need it to have you exactly as I want. You are mine."

"Never," the wench breathed. The sharp sensation in her nipple was matched by a clenching in her sex of a kind she had never felt before.

With a little moan, she realized the pirate was leaving the bed. The tight-fitting muslin shirt was already damp with sweat across the pirate's back, and the extravagant sleeves had lost their crisp appearance.

"Don't go," the wench finally said, when the pirate reached the door.

"You wish me to stay?"

Softly, the wench said, "Yes."

"Then don't worry, sweetheart. I've only a few matters of ship's business to attend to. We are only beginning the night, you and I."

The pirate's gaze traveled over the wench's stretched out form. Then she retraced her steps to stand over the bed. Removing her hat, she pulled the head scarf underneath off as well. She wound the silk in her hands, then leaned over the wench.

The wench could not have described the feelings that suffused her as the pirate tied the scarf around her head, covering her eyes. She did not anticipate the press of the pirate's mouth to hers, or the teasing fingers that came out of nowhere to pull firmly on her nipples.

"I want you to think about what I will do to you when I return. I want you completely focused on how I will make you mine. Why would I want you to surrender when conquering you will be more to my liking?"

The sound of the door closing ought to have relaxed the wench. The pirate was out of the room, and for the moment she was safe from demands on her body. But she could not relax. The pulsing between her legs only seemed to increase. Her mouth thirsted for another kiss. She pulled at the ropes only to ease the strain in her arms.

She did not want to be free.

She thought about the press of the pirate's body on hers—could, in truth, think of little else. She lost all track of time as she considered how a woman might satisfy her. She could not deny that she played the words *you are mine* over and over in her head.

The door opened and her body tightened in anticipation.

"Ah, I can see that you have been thinking." The pirate took note of the further hardened nipples and the legs that were more splayed than before. She pushed back the blindfold to look into the wench's eyes.

"Yes."

"That's the word I want to hear." The pirate, with a smug smile, straddled the silent woman's hips again. "Are you certain?"

The wench watched the pirate slowly draw her knife. "Yes."

The snick of the blade through fabric seemed louder than any words. The pirate held up a curl of ribbon. "I want to see all of you."

Snick. And again, until all the ribbons holding the chemise together were in the pirate's hand. She spilled them over the wench's body, then untied the sheath from her belt, slipped the knife in it and set it on the table next to the bed.

Their bodies seemed to glow, and the wench saw the pirate through the haze that darkened the harder her heart beat. But when their gazes locked the lust-drenched fog lifted, and she saw passion-fire leaping in the pirate's eyes.

The pirate bared her teeth. "My way, the way I've wanted you since the moment I laid eyes on you. Mine. Mine to enjoy."

The wench nearly cried out as the pirate tore apart what was left of her skirt. The strong hands shoved her legs open and she felt the press of something hard underneath the pirate's breeches against her sodden folds. This kiss was hard and deep and she could not help but moan when it ended, and the pirate's mouth moved down her body.

The smell of the wench's sex made the pirate's head spin. She was sweet like nothing else ever could be. She drove her tongue into the center of all that copious, thick wet and lapped up all of it she could, enjoying her spoils, relishing the richness of her treasure.

She used her lips, her teeth, her tongue, exploring, tasting, feasting on the luscious intimate flesh. Hers to enjoy. Hers to pleasure. Hers.

Her legs spread so wide she thought something would tear, the wench lifted her sex to the pirate's mouth again and again. She was possessed in an act so fiercely personal she could only respond with fervent, eager groans. She did not want it to stop, even after her pleasure peaked.

"Did you enjoy that, sweetheart?" The pirate knew the answer from the deep flush that stained the wench's chest and shoulders.

A fervent *yes* was trapped behind her lips. It was absurd to feel shy, but the sounds she'd made, the way she'd begged with her body—what would the pirate now think of the supposed lady she'd captured?

Fingers, sure and knowing, played over her sex. "It doesn't matter if you did or did not. I intend to do whatever I like with you. You are mine." The pirate stretched the full length of her to whisper in her ear. "Every inch of you, inside and out, is mine. A lady for my table, and a woman for my bed."

"Yes," the wench moaned. Fingers reached high inside her, moving hard and fast.

"You are mine, all of you. Do not think what I've already done made you mine. I've not begun to possess you." The pirate reveled in the response of the tender flesh she stroked. It trembled, as did the rest of the wench's luscious body, and she pushed in, again and again, until muscles yielded and the body under her writhed with pleasure. "I will enjoy you any way I like."

Twisting against the ropes, the wench could not help but use them to tighten herself under the pirate. She had never been touched thus, and the pleasure sending yellow starfire across her skin was terrifying.

"I would love one such as you, sometimes, but right now you want to be possessed, don't you?" The pirate kissed the gasping mouth as she felt the rolling hips jerk against her hand. "Admit it. Admit that you are mine and will ever be, and I will take you higher than your dreams."

The wench wanted to speak, but the shuddering in her sex would allow only harsh noises, animal noises. She was a lady, and she was not supposed to feel this way. She wasn't supposed to like it so much that she was glad of the ropes, glad they held her to the bed lest she fly in ecstasy.

"You want me to take my pleasure however I like as long as you feel this good, don't you? Spread your legs more for me. Your body was made for me to enjoy. Wet, delicious and mine."

Sensation forced a harsh cry, quickly echoed by the pirate.

"That's right, my sweet, like that. Open yourself. I love watching my hand on your hungry cunt, so red and wet and loving my hand back. Begging for more."

The pirate's voice came and went inside the wench's mind. Her flesh was trembling and quivering around the pirate's deeply thrust fingers, and there seemed no end to the wrenching, scorching tremors that shook her body.

Finally, she found her voice again, and again said the only word that mattered. "Yes."

The shifting bed drew her attention out of the well of sensation, and she gasped as the pirate withdrew her hand.

Slack-jawed, the pirate tweaked one nipple, then pinched harder, her breathing ragged. "I want more of you."

"Yes."

Untying the cord at her waist, the breeches fell down and the wench gasped again. Mesmerized, she watched the pirate caress the hard cock strapped to her loins with some liquid from the flask on the table.

"The oil of Venus, my sweet, will let my cock enjoy the inside of you for as long as I want." The pirate fell across the wench, spreading her legs. "I will take you for hours, take and enjoy your body, push into you over and over until I have had enough of you. It will be a long, long time before I am through, and believe me, my eager beauty, I will please you like no man ever could."

For a long moment, the pirate stared into the gleaming eyes, assessing the tears and slight lack of focus. Her wench was deeply aroused, of that she had no doubt. What surprised her was the depth of her own arousal at that moment. She did not want consent or encouragement. She wanted to conquer and take.

She might have hesitated a moment more, to be sure the wench was ready, but she did not. She wanted to enjoy this woman now, wanted her cock inside, wanted to feel the tender body beneath her moan and shiver all over again.

Without warning she rolled the wench onto her stomach, pushing her up the bed so the rope would give just enough as she lifted the gasping woman unceremoniously to her knees and elbows. She squeezed the dripping cunt, then greedily licked her fingers. Hers, all this passion was hers to savor.

Pillows stifled the scream the wench could not hold back. She was opened, taken, filled. When she had to draw breath she heard the pirate's crooning mixed with grunts as their dance became frantically mutual.

"I love watching my cock go inside you, the way you shove back and beg for more. Such a beautiful ass, shoulders." Squeezing, the pirate felt the wench's hips, her ribs, her shoulders. "Don't push me out, not yet. I've not fucked you enough. Move for me, dance for me, while I fuck you until you can't think."

The wench's groans tightened into a sharp cry as the pirate yanked hard on the waves of red curls. Her face came up out of the pillows, and she felt her cunt tighten, then swell.

"Mine," the pirate said fiercely. "After I've fucked you on your hands and knees, I will hold you down and fuck you while you dance under me."

"Yes!"

"You like it, don't you?"

"Yes!"

"Why—tell me why." The pirate shoved into her hard, then grasped the curving hips so she could shove in again.

"Yours. I'm yours." The truth was so much easier than pretending she hadn't always wanted to be mastered this way, exactly this way. "Because I'm yours to enjoy."

Something long unnamed and ignored in the pirate's mind began to shimmer with light. Her beautiful wench was crying with abandon, loving pleasure so fierce and intimate. Pirate she may be, but was she supposed to take such pleasure herself in her wench's helpless mewling, knowing her strength and insistence had overwhelmed this woman's natural reticence?

But wasn't this natural? Wasn't the way her body wanted this kind of love more natural than a high-toned lady's reluctance to admit she even had needs such as these? Her cunt ran like a river and her body rolled like an inexorable rising tide. Even so, was it permissible for the pirate to take such pleasure in it herself?

For a moment, the pirate found herself pausing, considering the heaving back now damp with sweat and the sob in the wench's voice.

"Don't stop! Please, please don't stop!" The wench tried to look over her shoulder, pleading in her broken voice.

The words were like burning rum igniting in the pirate's veins. The rasp of her own voice surprised her. "Get on your back, now."

The wench felt the pirate's firm hands turning her over, and she struggled with the ropes, dizzy with lust. She settled on her back as quickly as she could, so lost in desire that only a tiny voice asked what she must look like, tied to the bed, her hair in ruins, panting, legs spread and wanting nothing but more of whatever the pirate chose to give.

With a firm grip on the wench's legs, the pirate pulled her down until her arms were once again taut. "I am never going to stop doing this to you. Open for me."

When the wench's legs wrapped around the pirate's hips she was glad she'd not tied them down as well. More oil eased their coupling as they strained together, faster and faster.

"Are you strong enough?" The pirate arched with every thrust, loving the way the wench rose to meet her.

Eyes focused on the pirate's expression, the wench said through gritted teeth, "Are you?"

"God, woman, I will never let you go."

Her gaze near feverish with lust, the wench pulled hard on the ropes. "Do you think I want to go?"

Stretching, the pirate pulled the ends of her knots. In moments, the wench had freed her hands and with an earthy moan, wrapped her arms around the pirate's shoulders.

"I am yours," the wench said hoarsely. Her nails dug into the pirate's back. "And you are mine."

It could be no other way. The ship cleaves the ocean on its journey. As it yields, the ocean takes possession of the ship. The pirate sailed deeply into the wench's body, rising and falling until she knew no other rhythm.

Arms throbbing with their release, the wench grasped her knees and pulled them up, exposing herself completely to the pirate's taking. The pirate would and could take all, but there was power in giving everything. Panting and hoarse, they were covered in sweat. She wanted to take forever, give forever, but even as she tried to stay in that moment, she felt it wash away.

Ecstasy wrapped them in bonds neither could break. There was no boundary between give and take as they strained equally through the waves of pleasure that consumed them both.

Muslin pillowing her head, the wench slipped into exhausted sleep. With one hand curled in the tangle of red hair that spilled across the pillow, the pirate watched the delicate lashes flutter shut, then finally joined her dear wench in slumber as she thanked Mother Ocean for bringing this woman to her bed.

Stirring awake, the wench felt the reassuring warmth of her pirate's body next to her. The lamp had burned out and the cabin was washed in a hint of moonlight beyond the window curtains. A fold of muslin had drifted partially over her cheek. She pushed it away and sought out her pirate's face in the dark.

She had no doubt her pirate would be offended if told her features were delicate, but the wench thought it was thus. A tenderness beyond any she had ever felt filled her, and she touched the gentle chin with her fingertips.

Glancing down, she smiled and busied her fingers with the straps and buckles that had allowed her pirate to be so very vigorous earlier. She adored that inventive contraption, but her goal was the hidden treasure beneath.

The pirate stirred. "What are you—"

"Hush, pirate of mine." The wench kissed the soft, still sleep-tender mouth. She pushed away the leather and buckles, breeches . . . everything. "Oh . . ."

The pirate's eyes opened slightly. "Avast, wench."

The wench slipped a knowing two fingers into the cleft of her pirate's full, wet womanhood. "Now, do you mean stop, or hold fast?"

A shudder ran the length of the pirate's body, and the wench could not help a loving smile. "Thank you," she whispered, her fingers beginning a persistent flutter. "Thank you for this gift."

With a sharply indrawn breath, the pirate relaxed into the pleasure of the intimate touch. If she could take such pleasure in giving, why not from taking? Such a soft, easy stroke and the lips at her breast, nuzzling through the shirt, were equally intent.

"Am I pleasing you?" The wench closed her lips over the rising nipple she'd discovered through the crumpled muslin.

"Yes."

She used her teeth, just a little, and felt her pirate shiver. "I like that word."

"As do I. Your yeses set my blood on fire."

"Which ignites me more. Please, remove your shirt for me. I'm not wanting to stop my hand right now."

Her hands in a fever, the pirate pulled the snowy fabric over her head. The wench made a most satisfactory noise when the pirate completed the motion by pulling the wench's mouth to her breast. "Like that."

"Yes, my love."

They were both yes after that, yes to pleasure, yes to abandon. The pirate pulled the wench to her mouth for a hungry, panting kiss, followed by a groaned out, "Do not stop."

"It feels too good to stop." Her mouth bruised from passion, the wench gave kisses as fierce as she received. Her fingers were clenched high and tight as she ground her wet, swollen sex against the pirate's thigh. "I don't ever want to stop."

Steady, firm strokes from the wench's hand left the pirate gasping for breath. So needed and, after all that they had done together, so badly wanted. When the waves began she pulled the wench to her and their mutual cry was captured between their mouths.

Edges dissolved as soft laughter overtook them.

Close, sharing whispers and reassurances, they spooned under the quilt sleepily reclaimed from the floor.

When they woke from their mutual doze, the pirate helped her drowsy wench from the bed. "You are free."

Hair tangled and making no move to cover her naked body, the wench gave the pirate a smile the sun would envy. "Then I choose to stay."

The pirate opened the door and drew the wench to her so they could pass through it hand-in-hand.

"More water?" Jane proffered the bottle for the third time.

"I'm fine." Renee peered into the carton of cookie dough ice cream as she spooned up another bite. "God, this is divine."

"Here, let me." Jane took the carton and spoon and fed Renee another bite before having one herself. "Purely medicinal."

"Baby, I . . ." Renee accepted another bite, but abruptly wouldn't meet Jane's gaze.

"What?"

Renee shrugged, a vivid blush staining her shoulders and neck.

Alarmed, Jane set down the ice cream. "Did I hurt you? Oh honey, where? Was I too rough? Are you—"

Renee pressed her fingertips to Jane's lips. "No, no. You didn't hurt me. It was *wonderful*. Everything. It was all I fantasized about. I just . . ."

"What then?" Jane dizzily breathed in the scent on Renee's fingers.

"I needed so much," Renee whispered. "I didn't mean to take so long to be satisfied."

"Oh, hell, honey." Jane kissed the fingers still covering her lips. "I—I'm glad it took that long. I got really, really excited because you so needed everything I could do . . . you made me work. You were everything you could be, and that is such a turn on."

Renee's fingers trembled. "I was okay? Everything was good for you?"

Jane pushed the ice cream carton to one side, then gathered Renee fully into her arms. "You are everything to me, and being with you is always good. Always."

"Are you sure?"

"Darling." Jane tipped Renee's face up so she could look at her. "What? Why are you so shy all of a sudden?"

"Because, well . . . I was thinking . . ."

Jane felt the tickle of anticipation flutter in her stomach. The look on Renee's lovely face, the light in her eyes—they were always harbingers of wonderful things. "Hmm?"

"Pirates celebrate Thanksgiving, don't they?"

From Behind You Looked Like . . .

~1D~

Neenah and Ace knew everybody. That was, I reflected, the great thing about being one of their zillions of friends.

At every party I reconnected with everyone I'd lost touch with since the last party. It helped a lot to live down the hall from them—I got invited to every *soirée* they threw.

"Here, Parma." Ace handed me a paper cup full of a somewhat viscous red liquid.

"What on earth is that?"

"Ghoulicious Punch. My specialty."

"It looks like blood."

"It's Halloween. I love your costume, by the way. How'd you get the maggots to stick?"

I gave my best Corpse Bride titter. "It's a trade secret. I hope they come off again, though."

"Have someone help you," Ace said with concern. "That glue is close to the eye." She cocked her head. "I wonder who that is. Cute, very cute."

I followed her gaze to a petite Betty Boop emerging from the bathroom. She made a beeline for the ice chest of beers. "You're right about cute. I think I'm just old enough to be a dirty old woman these days because all I want to say is *nice Boopage.*"

Ace grunted agreement. "Too young for us."

"Speak for yourself. You're not old, you're just married."

"Same thing. And it's not like you've been dating much, so I'm not getting any vicarious thrills."

"I decided to give it a rest for a while. Sorry there's nothing to boast of." My shrug was nonchalant, I thought, but I didn't think Ace was convinced. There was no telling what Neenah had passed on from my months-ago drunken confession that I most emphatically had not let myself fall for a straight woman. I hadn't. I wouldn't. I'd gotten her out of my life and moved on.

"I'll tell Neenah you said being married made you old."

Ace gave me a mock look of horror as she wandered off.

"Hey, Parma. How did that condo deal work out for you?"

"Hi, Eve!" I gave my tax accountant a toothy grin. "It all fell through. You were right."

"I'm sorry I was. A condo in Hawaii would have been sweet." Eve mulled over the choice of cheeses and selected a cube of blue.

"I've got my eye on another place, but the way the market is right now I'm thinking I should wait." Oh, there was manchego.

We chatted for a while and Eve gave me oodles of free advice. I was her stockbroker and returned the favor. We'd just reached the point of solving all the problems with the existing tax code when someone jostled me.

"Sorry." Morticia Addams, her long face thick with chalk-white makeup, gave me an apologetic smile. "From behind you looked like someone I know."

"Are you saying I have someone else's ass?"

Eve laughed. "Or they have yours."

Morticia winked as she said, "Anyone would be lucky to have yours."

Oh my, flattery right off the bat. I adjusted my maggots. "How gallant of you, Morticia."

"Nice maggots."

"They're the talk of the party." I nodded at Eve as she drifted off. We were friends enough to know when to be scarce. "So, is there a Gomez?"

"No, but I'm looking for one." Her voice was a little husky, a quality I liked.

I sidled a little closer. Flirting is like breathing to me, and why not? It's like doubles tennis—find a good partner and stick with her for the length of a good game. "I'll call you Tish if that works for you."

"Later," she said. "Ask me later." She helped herself to a slice of California roll. "So, where's the Corpse Groom?"

"Alas, like you—no man in my life. Never has been."

"Ah, I envy you that. It took me a while to figure out I didn't need a Gomez."

"Not everybody sprang from Martina's forehead, in full rainbow gear."

"Really? It's taking a while for some people to stop calling me straight." She focused on the sushi, then selected another piece. "I notice you're not drinking the blood."

"Not my style. I was Elvira last year."

"You do have the figure for it."

I could tell a light blush was staining my skin. The last person to flirt with me this heavily had been that straight client with a serious case of seven-year itch. Willow had been mixed up about who she was—a very married woman. I might have let myself really care, but I was sure she'd go back to hubby eventually. I refused to be a cliché. Finally, for her sake of course, I'd had to make a clean break, referred her to another broker and stopped accepting her notes. None of it had hurt like hell. "You are a sweet talker. Maybe you should be Gomez."

"Oh, believe me, I'm very happy as a Morticia."

I gave her a steady look. "Do you carry a purse every day?"

She blinked. "Yes, why?"

"And you like that? Why don't you just put stuff in your pockets?"

She clearly thought I was insane, but answered, "Too much stuff. And when pockets are full it ruins the lines of the slacks."

"We're both femmes, then."

"Oh, I see. Purses and pockets?"

"It's nearly foolproof. See—look at that couple." I nodded toward a James Dean cuddling a black cat. "If Jimmy there had a purse it would look like she was holding either a football in protective custody or a dead raccoon at the end of her fingertips. Either way it would clearly be a case of her holding it until a femme returned for it. Ergo, butch."

Morticia laughed. "So the cat is a femme because she's got that adorable little shoulder bag? The rhinestone clip is gorgeous."

I leaned toward her and whispered, "I've never been that high a femme, though. I bet she has a bikini wax."

"I bet Jimmy's recently inspected that bikini wax."

We watched the two of them fondle each other. When the bathroom was vacated, they slipped in.

"I think we should go eavesdrop." Morticia's makeup was too thick for me to tell if she was blushing, but her dark eyes were twinkling with merriment and curiosity.

"You're a bad girl."

"I'm trying."

We didn't eavesdrop but when they emerged several minutes later, Jimmy's strut was even more pronounced. However, the cat, if anything, looked more frustrated. I was betting she yowled later.

"So what line of work are you in?" I nibbled on a sesame cracker, trying to figure out how old she was. The thick makeup made it hard to gauge.

"Let's not talk shop," she said quickly. "We could do that over coffee any day."

"What would you like to talk about?" I drew her toward the large picture window that looked onto Castro Street. "If I stand near the buffet any more I will eat a pound of the cheese."

"Do you play tennis or golf?"

"I golf."

"Really? I recently took it up. I have a terrible handicap—I can't hit the ball."

I laughed. "It takes practice. I played a round this morning, in fact. A group of women gets together once a quarter and plays a scramble for charity."

"That sounds like fun. I guess if I did it regularly, I'd get better."

The window sat above the street by about ten feet, but the extra lights were blocking most of the view. It happened every year. "Have you been outside?"

"No, not yet. I managed to get here through the crowd, and that gave me a bad case of claustrophobia."

"I had a short commute—from across the hall. How do you know Ace and Neenah?"

"I only know Neenah. We were introduced by a mutual friend a couple of months ago. When I bumped into her a few weeks ago, she was kind enough to invite me tonight."

"I'm glad she did." The words slipped out before I could catch them. But they were true. I knew I was blushing.

"Me too," she admitted shyly. "It's lovely to chat with you, Parma."

I realized then I didn't know her name. It was on the tip of my tongue to ask when Ace began proclaiming the beginning of the party games. That was normally my cue to exit.

"Do you like Pin-the-Tail-on-the-President?"

"I've never played."

151

"Parma," Ace called. "You have to play too."

"The blindfold will muss my maggots."

"Femmes," Ace scoffed. She appealed to Seven of Nine and Captain Janeway, who looked happy to play.

"She'll keep strong-arming me," I confided to Morticia. "I usually leave when the games begin."

"Oh." Morticia sounded gratifyingly disappointed. "Could we just step out for a while? Maybe watch the crowd outside?"

"We could go up to the roof."

"Oh, let's. I bet we can see the whole street."

We climbed the three flights and discovered the roof to be quite crowded. All of the possible positions overlooking the street were taken.

"Oh. I had no idea."

"The air feels good," Morticia said. "Let's stay up here."

I was about to ask her for her real name, when she said, "I am new at this, I will admit it, but I'm determined to somehow become a bona fide lesbian, as soon as possible. How do I let a woman know I'm available?"

"Same way you'd let a guy know." I leaned against the access door. "You could just say it. Is there someone?" I congratulated myself on being able to casually ask the question, but I was going to be disappointed if she said yes.

She looked at me, her face in the shadows. Her voice lost its husky edge. "She couldn't get over the fact that when we met I was straight. She's the reason why I figured out I wasn't straight at all. She—well, we reached a kind of turning point. And she said she'd been hurt by someone who had said she was gay, but then went back to her husband. So . . . I don't know how to tell her I'm divorced now."

"You could drop her a note."

"I tried. She's not accepting my e-mails anymore."

"Oh, that's a bit harsh." I tried to be more sympathetic, but a big part of me was bummed that the flirting had stopped, and now I was Ann Landers.

"No, I was really intense and was having a hard time accepting no. She'd tell me we had to stick to business, but I always got her to talk about other things."

"Maybe you should figure out a way to cross her path."

"I did."

"And?"

"Don't know yet. I think she likes me, though. I think she wanted to like me a lot more than she let on."

"How can you be sure?"

"We kissed. I don't mean we kissed, I mean we *kissed*. For hours sometimes. It was world-class."

Willow had been a first-class kisser, I reflected, not that I was going to go maudlin and miss her. "You could try that again."

"I suppose she might slap me."

Sighing inwardly, I blithely advised, "Just grab her and see what happens."

Morticia moved abruptly, taking a firm hold of my shoulders. "Okay."

She kissed me.

I was so surprised I didn't even let out a squeak. I had long enough to wonder what I ought to do—let the kiss end gracefully or knee her? But I came to no decision. The kiss ended when she sighed. That's when I realized I'd slipped my arms around her waist as if that was the most natural thing in the world.

The light was dim, but not so much so that I couldn't see into those dark eyes. Those familiar dark eyes. "Willow?"

"Yes, Parma." She kissed me again, and that was all I thought about—her sweet lips, her incredibly supple tongue. She was right, we had made out for hours without going any further. It had been maddening and sexy and tempting. I'd walked around in a daze, feeling beautiful and desired and yet strung out because I couldn't say yes when I was certain that, eventually, she would hurt me.

"You're divorced?"

"Nearly, but there's no going back. I told him why I was leaving and wished him a good life. I was going to drop by your office, very casually, and try to tell you, but I ran into Neenah and after I told her, she invited me tonight."

"That's typical of her." Matchmaker Neenah—it made sense.

"I'm sorry."

"You've nothing to be sorry for. You told me you were going to come out."

"But until I did how could you believe me?"

"I believe you now." I pulled her close, and she gathered me up in her long arms. "That makeup job is amazing. You don't look at all like you."

"I'd like to take it off, to tell the truth."

Feeling shy, I said, "Why don't you use my bathroom?"

She nodded and kissed me again.

My arms tightened around her, and I was amazed at how we fit. There have been women I didn't fit with well at all. But Willow and I matched up where all the curvy places could get quite close. I loved curvy places on women.

As I led the way back down the stairs I wasn't thinking we'd go to bed. I wasn't letting myself think it. She wasn't a sexual novice, she'd admitted that, but I'd be her first woman. What was the word for it? Willow was *re-virginated*. That scared me.

I got out the cold cream and several washcloths and left her to it. In the bedroom I quickly tossed my dirty laundry into the closet and made the bed. Using the bedroom mirror, I began peeling off my own bits and pieces. Time for the maggots to go.

She was patting her face dry as she studied it in the mirror when I joined her again. I reached for the jar of cold cream. "My turn."

Our reflections shared a smile. It was Willow, all right. The eyes I should have recognized, but now her nose didn't look so long, and her normally ruddy cheeks were even more reddened after the scrubbing. "That really was some makeup job."

The huskiness she must have feigned was completely gone. I didn't really miss it, though. "Thanks. I was afraid you'd be mad."

"Well," I allowed, "if you'd actually seduced me and only then revealed yourself, I might have been."

"Is that a possibility?" She turned to face me. "Could I seduce you?"

I didn't know what to say. The answer from places not my brain was a loud *yes*. But my brain was thinking we ought to move slower than that.

"Sorry," she said quickly. "I'm getting ahead of things. I've wanted you for all the years we had those quarterly meetings, that's all. I can wait a little while longer."

She ceded the place over the sink, and I went to work on my face. With a layer of white goo on it, I felt for some reason a little emboldened. "It's not that I didn't want to. You know how much." If not for the cream she'd have seen a blush.

"Parma, I can wait a little while longer."

For some reason, her calm irked me. I scrubbed at the spirit gum dotted on my face in several places. Fine, I thought. "Could you unzip my dress for me? The zip sticks, and I've been worried about being able to get it off."

I enjoyed the not-very-calm expression deep in her eyes. The cool air on my back felt very nice. I wasn't wearing a bra. From her startled gasp, I gathered she hadn't realized.

I bent over the sink to scoop water onto my face. The shroud-cum-wedding dress drooped forward, and I could feel more cool air, this time on my ass. I've always liked boy shorts with lace.

"I'll wait out here," Willow said.

By the time my face was clean I had the well-scrubbed look of a schoolchild. It wasn't exactly the sexual predator I had been hoping for. So she wanted to wait? Well, what if I didn't?

I'd turn the lights down, and maybe my scrubbed face wouldn't matter so much.

Ineptly clutching my dress to my front, I joined her in the living room. "Would you like some tea?"

She didn't answer.

Oops, I lost my grip on the shroud. My right breast was exposed for several moments, darn it. "Sorry. Tea?"

"I should go."

"Right this moment?"

"Parma, I'm going to jump on you if I stay another minute." She was halfway to the door already.

"So, now that I've thought about it, okay."

"Huh?" She swung round to face me, her eyes wide. "Just like that?"

"Yeah. We've waited long enough."

"Parma, please don't tease me."

I worked my index fingers under the lacy waistband of my boy shorts. "Willow, I haven't begun to tease you."

She was breathing hard—at least I thought she was. Her gaze was glued to my fingers. I ran them back and forth, slowly revealing my abdomen. Soon, she'd know I had a few gray hairs.

"Parma?"

"Hmm?"

"I have no idea what to do."

"I do."

She took a long, shaky breath as well as several steps toward me. "Can I touch you?"

I closed the distance and took her hands in mine. So much for the shroud. "Yes. Please do."

The shiver that ran through her body was fierce and fast. "I want to really touch you."

"Really touch me, please." I put her hands on my breasts.

"God. Oh, Parma."

"Don't cry." I stepped into her embrace. "Sweetie, everything is going to be wonderful."

She put her arms around my bare back. "I know it will be. I'm scared."

"There's no mystery. I'm built just like you."

"That's not it," she said hoarsely. "I'm afraid I'm going to hurt you when I do this."

She kissed me hard, hungrily and her hands gripped me so tightly I knew I would bruise. I wound my hands in her long, black hair, and it felt like we were back on my office couch, the last time we'd made out. My skin was hot, but this time I didn't have to constantly tell myself to keep my hands above her waist.

I got her dress off of her, though her desire to continue kissing me slowed down the process. When she was naked—wonderfully, completely naked for me—I kissed her to the couch, and we fell on it. I was on top, which I liked.

"We've waited long enough," I said. "More than long enough for this."

She moaned sharp and hard when my hand went between her legs. Oh, yes, I thought. I'd known when we were on the office couch that she was like that. I'd known she wanted me. I just hadn't wanted my heart to get more hurt than it was going to be when she eventually dumped me.

"You're so ready," I whispered, kissing her throat. "Let's go fast, then we'll go really, really slowly. And do everything."

She managed a half-laugh. "You always were good at teaching me."

"I think by the time we get to morning, you'll be teaching me."

I opened her lips with two fingers, and brushed over her very hard, very eager clit. Rubbing along both sides of it, I listened to her gasps and moans and coos, and concentrated on the shifting in her hips. Her shoulders arched back and then I heard that sharpening moan and her pelvis tipped up. It was all the invitation I needed when she was also now groaning out, "Yes."

I slipped those wet two fingers inside her, not too hard, but firmly. Her legs went limp as I steadily moved in, out, back in. I was memorizing the inside of her because I wanted to know the way next time, and the next. I wanted lots of next times. This was Willow, I told myself. I was making love to Willow the way I'd fantasized over and over.

"Do you want my mouth?"

"God, yes. Please, Parma. God, yes."

I moved down to look at her, gleaming and open. Beautiful. I'd known she'd be beautiful here, too. I kissed her clit wetly, then rubbed it with my lips. Simply beautiful.

She cried out the moment my mouth was on her, then again just moments later. Muscles inside her clenched up, and I fluttered my fingers to make sure she could feel me there. I sucked her clit between my lips and flicked it with my tongue, loving her cries and how wet she got all over again.

This was Willow, and I'd known she'd be like this.

She stroked my hair as I rested my head on her tummy. "I had no idea. Really. I knew it would feel good, but I had no idea."

"You're very responsive." It's Willow, I thought again, and my sense of wonder continued to grow. I smiled to myself. I hadn't wanted to admit my heartbreak, but something must have been broken when I could feel so whole now.

"You're awfully good at that."

"You're delicious to taste."

"The things you say." She gently pulled my hair for a moment.

"I think mutual admiration is important to a relationship, don't you?"

I heard the little laugh through her tummy. "What do you say to us having a real date?"

"Not tonight," I said.

"Oh."

I raised my head and gazed into her eyes. "Tomorrow. Tonight I just want to take you to bed."

"Oh." She made a show of thinking it over. "Okay. But on one condition."

"Name it."

"That what you just did to me I get to do to you."

"Oh sweetie," I said, one eyebrow raised. "Like I'm going to try and stop you."

She was slow and gentle with me, hands gliding over my back and shoulders. We kissed again, languidly, and I sensed part of her hesitation was being not quite sure what to do.

"It'll be fine," I said between kisses.

"I want to make you feel wonderful."

"Why don't we move to the bedroom?" I kissed her one last time, pulled her up from the sofa, then kissed her again. By the time we moved to the bed she was kissing me with little nips and moans that left me in no doubt at all that she wanted me.

"I'm going to leave the lights on," I whispered. I knew the light would help her find the right places, but it also meant I could watch her and that little ballerina pirouetting in my stomach could go right on singing, "It's Willow, it's Willow."

She kissed my neck, my shoulders. Her tongue wound around my nipples with the same supple care with which she'd caressed my mouth. Willow was making love to me, and I wanted to put the heartache away and lose myself in this experience. Maybe my heart was still guarded, but my body need not be, not right now, not when she was looking between my legs as if I was the most beautiful sight she'd ever seen.

"Parma, I . . ." She raised her gaze to my eyes and seemed unable to move.

I touched her cheek with my fingertips, then tipped her head down to look between my legs again. Slowly, as I said, "It'll be okay," I opened my lips and slipped one finger between them, gliding easily through an ocean of wet.

Her arms were shaking. "God, Parma, I feel as if I'm going to explode."

I continued parting the salt-and-pepper hair that, had I known, I would have trimmed more carefully. Had I known Willow would come into my life again, I would have shaved my legs and kept up the extra work with the free weights. Clearly, though, she liked what she saw, and I felt beautiful for her.

When I lifted my glistening finger to her mouth she shuddered. She let me push my finger between her lips and yet it was a long moment before her tongue touched it. Finally, her tongue swept the tip, and she made a noise of passion I'd not yet heard from her, but oh, I hoped to hear it again and again. Her eyes shimmered with tears as she sucked and tasted, then she pushed my legs farther apart and, after a deep breath, buried her face there.

The noise I made was one I'd not heard before either. She explored me with care, her tongue sliding and slipping and curling all through my folds. She pushed, licked, tickled, then lifted her face to grin at me.

"What?" She looked absolutely delighted.

"It's wonderful, Parma. Is it okay that I'm really liking this?"

I had to laugh. "We're women." I touched her face. "We're lesbians. And we get to enjoy this as often as we like."

"Yes," she breathed out just before she lost the smile and her eyes focused again between my legs. Settling onto her tummy, she eased my lips apart with her hand and said with a little gasp, "I like this especially."

She kissed my clit with a kind of reverence, kissed it again and again. Her tongue flicked it, and I let out a yelp that surprised both of us. Clearly alarmed, she asked, "Did I hurt you?"

160

"God no, just do that again." I touched the side of her head. "Do that again, and again, and—God, Willow, don't stop."

She pressed her mouth hard into me and I must have swooned. Me, the one who knew what to do was nearly senseless as she pushed my knees to my breasts and kept doing that wonderful thing with her tongue. I cupped my breasts and made cooing sounds that might have been the calling of birds because I was flying, and it was Willow lifting me up so high.

I came, I know I did, but that fact was secondary to the sound of her ragged breathing as she sobbed into my thigh. I tried to focus, but breathing was more important.

When I stopped seeing everything through a haze of sparkling magenta, I could finally hear what she was saying.

"Forgive me . . . I didn't know . . ."

"Know what, sweetie?" I found enough energy to prop myself up onto my elbows. "I have nothing to forgive you for."

"I tormented you for all those months. Tried to get you to go across the line so all I had to do was let it happen. I tormented you, and I didn't know what an *amazing* thing you had the strength to say no to. If I had known that tasting you and feeling you come against my mouth would be so beautiful I'd have begged." She gasped for air even as I tried to shush her. "How did you say no? I know you wanted me, and you knew how intense and incredible it was—"

"Willow, sweetheart, I'm not some stoic masochist. I only said no because I thought I'd get hurt." I stroked her wet cheek. "I knew I would adore making love to you. I dreamed night after night about you doing what you just did. God, I was crazy wanting you." All the things I hadn't told anyone—not even myself—poured out of me. "But I think we're all born liking certain things and just because you like tasting me didn't mean you didn't like what you already had with him." Like social acceptance, I wanted to add, and joint tax returns and all the things I could not give her.

161

She kissed the fingertips I pressed to her lips. "I'll admit at first I couldn't see anything happening between us that wasn't an affair. I knew I loved you like nothing ever before and yet I wasn't—"

"Sweetie," I interrupted softly. "We can talk about this for as long as you like, and I promise we will."

"I have a world of things to tell you."

"Me, too, you." I pulled her up into my arms. "The first of which is that I am suddenly very, very sleepy. And I want to wake up in your arms."

She blinked at me. "I was trying hard not to show it. I feel I could sleep a week."

I laughed fondly. "We have lots to learn. And lots of time?" I didn't mean it like a question but it came out that way. In spite of her warmth against me I felt vulnerable and exposed.

"Lots of time. As much as we need. Sweetheart," she added shyly.

To be honest, I fell asleep first, but it was only by a few minutes. I stirred in the night and so did she.

But no matter how we turned we were touching and the little ballerina pirouetting in my stomach did not stop singing, "It's Willow, it's Willow."

Chosen

~1B~

"That reminds me of the time I was working the late shift at Mickey D's."

Gwen gave Sheila a withering look. "Everything reminds you of the late shift at Mickey D's."

"You can base your entire theory of life on Mickey D's."

Sheila was baiting Gwen now, and Erika knew it wouldn't be long until there was blood in the water. It seemed like a good time to announce, "I'm going to get laid tonight."

"How exactly will you do that, pad'nuh?" Sheila tweaked her handlebar mustache. "I think you're supposed to have a bandanna or something."

Erika adjusted the purple-and-white cheerleader outfit and wished she'd worn tights for warmth. "Even so, I think I won't have much trouble finding someone. This is the Castro, isn't it?"

"You've never done anything like that before." Gwen touched Erika's arm. "You need to be safe."

"What could happen?" Suddenly, Erika couldn't wait to get away from the two of them. She'd been watching Gwen make eyes at Sheila all night, then picking little fights as if they were on a grade school playground. A fool could tell Gwen was dripping for Sheila lately, and Erika didn't want to watch Sheila get the girl one more time. If there was one thing Erika devoutly hoped, it was that she didn't look as lovesick as Gwen did. She had some pride. A little. If Sheila was finally going to play with Gwen, it was time Sheila realized good little Erika could play too. "I'm going to prowl, I'm going to get laid and that's all there is to it."

Sheila looked highly skeptical. "Get out. You have never one-nighted in your life. You need to do that love thing before you'll even French kiss."

"She's right," Gwen said. "Don't be a child about sex."

"I'm not a child," she contested hotly. "I have so had one-nighters."

"Not that you intended. You thought they'd all call you later."

Tears stung Erika's eyes, and without another word she walked away. Clinging to some kind of standards hadn't gotten her Sheila, and maybe becoming the kind of girl Sheila liked to party with was the only way. She would just stop hoping for a life and instead be too cool to think sex and love could go together.

She wanted Sheila out of her head tonight, especially if Gwen and Sheila went home together. *I need to get laid. I need to get laid tonight.*

She paused under a street light to rub her bare thigh. The bona fide slayer wooden stake and dagger that hung around her cheerleading skirt were heavy and abrasive. Sheila has insisted on the real thing, but they were going to rub a hole in her leg. Maybe if she switched them with the poms she'd be more comfortable.

Her outfit adjusted more to her liking, she was most of the way to Castro Street when a dark-cloaked form stepped out in front of her. She couldn't help a startled cry.

"I'm sorry," a low, melodious voice said. "I didn't mean to frighten you."

"I'm not frightened," Erika answered. "It was unexpected, that's all." She stepped around the tall figure with her head held high.

"I'm still sorry. I don't like to startle beautiful women."

They'd passed under a street light, and Erika was able to see the woman more clearly. "Not when I've got all the weapons I need to slay you," Erika teased. Then she glanced at the stranger's face. Her first thought was *wow* and her next was no more coherent.

Dark, luminous eyes regarded her with some amusement, and for just a moment Erika felt like a delicious morsel on a platter. The vampire cape, draped heavily over broad shoulders, shrouded the tall figure in black. The cloak's stand-up collar circled the woman's head, highlighting those incredible eyes.

Finally, with a quirky smile, the woman said, "I know I ought to be frightened of a genuine vampire slayer, but I think I'll risk it tonight."

After a nervous swallow, Erika managed to say, "It's Halloween—maybe we can declare a truce."

"A wonderful idea. And your name?" The woman extended her arm, and Erika felt perfectly natural tucking her hand into the crook.

"Erika. How about you?" She was pleased that this elegant woman thought they made a fitting couple.

"Dina." She patted Erika's hand with her own, walking them both up the street.

Dina's cape must have cost a fortune, Erika mused. It was heavy, like thick velvet but lined with something crimson and silky. *Duh, like maybe it's silk for real.* "Pleased to meet you, Dina."

"Charmed." The simplicity of the word made Erika feel like royalty. She couldn't place Dina's accent, either. Something European, but not British or German.

"Where are we heading?"

"I was walking toward the block party, hoping to stroll with someone lovely on my arm," Dina said.

"Oh." Erika groaned inwardly, realizing she sounded like a geek. "Me too."

"Then we'll go together, shall we?"

Erika felt lighter than air. Would it be so terrible and so dangerous if she let Dina lead her down one of the little alleys? The one they'd just passed had secreted not one but two pairs of lovers. It could be quick and easy. And maybe Dina would call tomorrow . . .

Stop that, she chided herself. You're just trying to get something for tonight, so you can tell Sheila and Gwen that you did. So Sheila will realize you like sex.

Dina was smiling slightly, as if some inner thought provided light amusement. She was strong, Erika thought. Her arm felt like steel.

"There is something I need to take care of," Dina said as they rounded the last corner to Castro Street. The crowd seemed to naturally part for them. "It won't take a minute."

"I'd be happy to wait."

"That would be perfect." Dina stopped in front of an apartment building. Erika shook her head slightly, then realized Dina was holding the door open. "Would you like to wait in the lobby? I'm showing a vacant apartment in the morning and I just want to make sure it's still tidy."

Erika ducked her head shyly as she preceded Dina into the building. The hubbub of a loud party was the first thing she noticed. The second was that Dina moved very quickly. She had thought Dina had been behind her, but she was already halfway up the stairs to the first floor landing. *I could really get lost in her.*

Dina turned midway up the stairs, and that little smile was back. She didn't say anything, but her head tipped slightly. "I could practice by showing it to you."

168

Erika took a deep breath. Why was she so dizzy now? She scurried across the lobby in Dina's wake.

Dina's cape spread out behind her as she moved quickly up the stairs. Erika fancied she saw something like sparks flow from it. She hurried to keep up, more than slightly out of breath.

Dina was already at the door to apartment 1B before Erika had climbed the half-flight. For a moment, she looked past Dina to the open door of another apartment, the one where all the music and noise was coming from. Then she could look at nothing but Dina, who stepped back so Erika could precede her into the apartment.

"You can take a look around, if you want." Dina was like some magician, Erika thought. Whatever keys she'd used had opened the door without a clink or scrape.

"I'd love to." Of her own free will she walked into the apartment. Glancing over her shoulder, she saw Dina just outside the door, framed in the light.

With a courtly half-bow, Dina said teasingly, "May I come in, my lady?"

"Please do." Erika shuddered at the smile of pure electricity that Dina gave her as she stepped over the threshold.

The door closed, though Erika did not see it swing shut, and there was no light except a soft glow behind her. She turned, frightened and curious, and saw Dina was the source of the light, already standing on the other side of the empty living room. She must have painted herself with glow-in-the-dark solution, Erika thought. It was very cool.

Dina was staring at her, and Erika didn't know what to say. She felt a prisoner to those hungry, intense eyes that seemed even brighter in the low light. "Yes, Erika," Dina murmured. "I can do the same for you, if you like."

"Oh, I'd love it." She rubbed her arms to stave off the chill of the room.

"I'm sure you will." Dina arched one eyebrow. Her smile was broad and broken by the flick of her tongue over her lips. "I knew you'd love it the moment I saw you."

"You did?" In Erika's opinion, Dina was entirely too far away. The craving for their bodies to meet became an urgent pulse behind her eyes.

"I did." Dina walked by Erika, leaving behind a complicated cologne. As Erika watched, Dina brushed a hand near the fireplace and flames suddenly came to life. Erika thought if she could ever afford a place like this, she'd want an instant starter just like that. She and a lover could get right down to business. Any moment she was sure she'd feel the warmth.

Dina was staring at her, with that little smile. She seemed to be waiting for Erika to say or do something.

"It's a great apartment."

"It would be easier to find occupants if it was furnished." Dina made a little gesture, and Erika looked around her.

There was no furniture at all. Did that go for the bedroom too? She was disappointed. She'd been certain that Dina had brought her here to seduce her, but on the cold floor?

"It *is* cold," Dina murmured.

Could Dina read her mind? You're just being freaky, Erika told herself. She made herself walk toward the kitchen. Why didn't Dina turn on the rest of the lights, though?

Trying hard not to look eager, she left the dim kitchen, which she could remember nothing about two seconds later, and turned toward the closer of two bedrooms. Even in the low light from the fire, she could tell it was empty. So was the second one.

Dina was right behind her when she turned back to the living room.

"How do you do that?"

"What?"

"Move so quickly and quietly?"

"A great deal of practice."

Dina didn't move out of the doorway, and the pounding of Erika's heart grew louder and louder.

She didn't remember moving into Dina's arms. The kisses were slow and intimate. Dina's tongue firmly explored her mouth and Erika found herself gasping for breath. She wanted to somehow become one with Dina, the way she'd always known she'd be with Sheila. The thought of Sheila was jarring, though, as if what Dina offered and what she'd find with Sheila were not at all the same thing.

"That's right," Dina whispered. "We will be one."

"Yes," Erika moaned. "That's what I want."

"You are chosen. My chosen."

Erika swooned when Dina's mouth nuzzled her throat. She wanted to be consumed—that was the right word for it. All these years she'd wanted to be the one Sheila played with, the one who could keep up with whatever Sheila wanted right then. Tonight she would be Dina's plaything instead, and it was Sheila's loss.

Disoriented, she could only grasp that Dina was carrying her someplace, but she couldn't do anything about it. She was on something soft, like a bed, but where could it have come from?

Dina's mouth was at her throat again. Her cloak covered Erika almost completely. She was burning with a ceaseless desire for union. Dina pulled up Erika's sweater, and Erika felt that insistent tongue licking at her nipples. Her entire body trembled. She had wanted this, hadn't she? Yes, she'd wanted to get laid, but suddenly there seemed to be so much more happening.

Sharp teeth grasped her nipple and she groaned even as she tried to push Dina away. "Stop."

"Chosen one, on this holy night." Dina bit her again and a wave of arousal made Erika feel as if she was drowning.

"Please, no."

"Too late. Once chosen, we must conclude our union."

This was just some freaked out game, Erika thought. There's something in her cologne to make me feel like I can't move. She tried to speak more firmly. "Stop, Dina. I want to stop."

Dina laughed and bit her again, nearly breaking the skin.

Erika's terror exploded against the inside of her head. It was an awful feeling, being so afraid that she couldn't move or scream. She could feel Dina's hand fumbling with her skirt and what was worse, part of her still wanted Dina to do that. She wanted it all, and yet she was so scared she was seeing nothing but silver white mist in the air around them.

The mist closed in on them while Erika tried to scream. It was cold but Erika had impressions of rolling blue ocean, a scent like sweet wine and then laughter, like lovers sharing their hearts. No, it's just a trick of light, she told herself, but she was less afraid with the mist there. You are freaking out, another part of her answered, and there's nobody here to save you but you.

Dina threw her head back with an angry growl, shrugging her shoulders as if the mist burned instead of chilled. Instead of a soft bed under her, Erika now felt the cold hardwood floor. Dina's eyes went red, and she slapped at the congealing mist, now slowly turning her skin to frozen silver. The growl in Dina's throat intensified as she sprang to her feet, clutching Erika's wrist. Then the mist enveloped her completely and the grip on Erika's wrist became painful.

"Now," something whispered inside her head. "Now, while I can still hold her."

Erika pulled frantically on her wrist, but Dina's grip was like iron. Fumbling with her free hand, she drew the dagger, but the plastic blade had no impact on Dina, whose fingers seemed to shred the mist. The poms, she thought hysterically, but her hand closed on the stake. Without a second thought she slugged Dina in the gut with the point, hard, and had a vague impression of dust all over her hands, then she was free, suddenly out in the common hallway, frantically pulling down her sweater. Down the stairs, out the door, into the still crowded street. She was sobbing for breath and never so glad to see so many people before in her life.

"Erika!" Sheila, moustache and cowboy hat askew, grabbed her arm. "Where'd you go? You scared the shit out of me."

Erika looked back at the apartment building. There was no sign of Dina. "I'm okay," she said shakily. "I just got scared, that's all."

"Well, it's scary out here. It's getting pretty late, and I think we should stick together." She pulled Erika against her. "Don't do that to me. I had this feeling something terrible had happened to you."

It was the easiest thing in the world to put her arms around Sheila and soak in the safety. Erika didn't know what to think of Dina's freakish behavior. She felt stupid for having gone anywhere with a stranger—but wasn't that what she'd said she'd planned on doing? Reality had been far, far different than fantasy.

But had it even happened? She'd felt dizzy and disoriented . . . maybe she'd wandered into that building, got a huge hit of second-hand pot or something and imagined it all. Dina hadn't been real. None of it had happened. But she wasn't going back to look for the dagger and stake no longer swinging at her side— they could be easily replaced if she wanted to be a slayer again next year.

She wasn't going to leave the safety of Sheila's arms. Sheila was real. The concern in Sheila's eyes was real. Right then all that mattered to her was the warmth of Sheila's arms around her.

Gwen said, over her shoulder, "I think you got too much sun on our hike earlier."

"No, I've just got a chill," Erika said for the umpteenth time. "I'm sorry you have to leave on my account."

"That street party was over, the fun bit at least." Sheila tightened her arm around Erika as they snuggled in the backseat of Gwen's car. "You're still shivering."

"It's your moustache," Erika lied, though the moustache did tickle.

"That's easy to fix." Sheila didn't even flinch as she peeled the handlebars off her lip.

Feeling silly, Erika said quietly, "I think I met a vampire."

Sheila didn't laugh. "Or something equally scary?"

Erika nodded, then glanced warily at Gwen. "I guess I'm not the one-night stand type after all."

"It's not all it's cracked up to be," Sheila said softly. "It has its limitations, especially if your heart's somewhere else."

Very softly, trying to understand what Sheila's eyes seemed to be saying, Erika asked, "Like where?"

Leaning close, Sheila whispered in her ear, "With someone who thinks you're a buddy. Who thinks you're into easy sex and no tomorrow."

Erika thought her heart had stopped beating. "Sheila . . . ?"

Sheila pulled her head back and the lights of approaching cars flicked over her serious expression, rendering her in light, dark, light, dark. Her lips parted as if she was going to say something but she only nodded.

"Really?" Erika shivered again, finally feeling the warmth of Sheila's body throughout her own. *Please let this moment be real.* "Why . . . ? I mean, why tell me tonight?"

"I had this horrible feeling you were dead." Sheila shrugged, but it was not an easy motion. "It was freaky creepy. And I thought how stupid, if I never saw you again, how stupid not to tell you how I felt. Even if you laughed."

"I'm not laughing," Erika said slowly.

Sheila took her hand and, for the rest of the drive, didn't let go.

❧

174

She'd seen party-bad-girl Sheila stalk women with the brooding eyes and you're-the-one smile. Watched her push a more-than-willing woman against a wall with just enough force to elicit a moan from her partner—and a silent one from Erika as well. In late-night, alcohol-inspired confessions, she'd heard about ropes and toys and three-ways, and involved tales of Anything Goes.

What surprised her, when Sheila and she stood just behind the closed door of Sheila's apartment, was the tenderness in Sheila's face. The sweetness of the smile. The tiny tremor of her hands that might have meant—to Erika's surprised delight—that Sheila was nervous. It was true that she craved a time when Sheila would handle her just a little rough, but right now she needed gentleness. She'd learned a valuable lesson tonight—fear did not turn her on.

She couldn't help but smile as Sheila slowly traced her cheekbones with a trembling index finger.

Sheila cocked her head. "What?"

"You. This isn't what I expected."

"What did you expect?"

She began to shrug but Sheila's intense look begged for an honest answer. "That if you wanted me you'd have tied me up and fucked me a long time ago."

"I don't want to fuck you, baby." Sheila leaned close enough that her breath warmed Erika's lips. "I want to make love to you. That includes fucking. But it also includes this," she finished as her hands firmly grasped Erika's shoulders.

"Yes," was all Erika managed to say before Sheila kissed her.

The press of Sheila's lips was almost chaste. Erika hadn't realized there was so much to explore in a kiss. Firm, then yielding, soft, moist, then suddenly wet and gasping. Finally, Sheila carefully cupped the back of Erika's neck. Erika's lips parted in response, and Sheila tasted her in slow, sensuous exploration. They shared a mutual moan between their mouths and for a long, long time, just that was enough.

175

Sheila was the one who smiled into their kiss, and it was Erika's turn to ask, "What?"

"I've never danced with you."

Erika realized they were slowly moving against each other, an intimate dance that so far didn't want to speed up. "I'm enjoying it."

"God, you're a great kisser."

"Really?" Erika had never been told that before.

"Uh-huh," Sheila said before beginning another long, sensual kiss.

Erika could have stayed right there, in that moment, forever. These kisses had none of the complications of passion and all of the reassurance of pleasure. After her terror earlier in the evening, being held close and kissed this way by Sheila seemed the perfect antidote.

She drew Sheila to the sofa after a while, where it made sense to stretch out and pull Sheila down on top of her. They kissed. And they kissed. But in that position the slow easy movement of their hips created heat. Eventually, Erika was aware that the spectacular kisses that seemed to light up her soul were no longer enough.

Sheila had for the longest time only one leg between Erika's, and Erika didn't know when that had changed. Her thighs were wrapped around Sheila's chaps and the tingles reminded her that her skin was bare and it liked very much to be touched. If she arched just right it felt very, very good in all the best places.

"You're going right to my head," Sheila whispered. "Where did you learn to kiss like this?"

"I think you bring out the kisser in me."

"You're delicious. And playful. It makes me want . . ."

"Want what?" Please say it, Erika wanted to beg. Just say that you want me, want to enjoy me.

"Sometimes I can get carried away and be bad. I know what I'd like to do right now but not if you're still feeling—"

"No, I'm fine. You can . . ." Have me, Erika wanted to say.

Have me, love me, take me, do whatever you want to me. Couldn't Sheila tell how much Erika wanted to be hers?

"Why, baby?"

"Because . . . I've loved you forever."

"And you want me to touch you?"

"Yes . . . God!" Erika stiffened against Sheila's hand, which had slipped between them. Lightly, gently, Sheila's fingers played over the thin black panties Erika had chosen for under the pleated skirt. The light touch made her tighten in anticipation of more.

"Why, baby?"

"Because I love you. And I trust you and want to be with you."

"But why do you want me to touch you?" Sheila lifted her head so she could look into Erika's eyes. "It's simple."

"I need you, Sheila. I need you, and everything feels right with you."

"Too many words." Sheila kissed her, hard and swift, while her fingers kept up the teasing play over Erika's panties. "You know why you want me to touch you. I just want to hear you say it."

What more was there to say? Erika searched the years of their friendship and all the reviews Sheila had given her of the various women she'd been with. What did Sheila want to hear? What more was there than love, desire, need?

She'd been silent too long, because Sheila kissed her again and said, softly, "It's very simple right now. We're both turned on, and we want to feel good together, love each other, don't we?"

Erika breathed out, "Yes."

"You want me to touch you, do anything to you . . ."

"God, yes."

"Because you want me to make you come. That's everything right now."

"I would have thought it was obvious." Erika strained against

Sheila's body, trying to feel more of Sheila's fingers against her skin.

"You'd be surprised. I've kissed women who didn't want to come, let alone for me, but the kisses were good. I can touch a woman for hours and if she doesn't come we haven't . . ." Sheila shrugged. "I know some people don't agree, but if she doesn't come I don't feel like we really . . . fucked. It could be a hell of a lot of fun, but it doesn't count."

"I want it to count," Erika whispered, capturing Sheila's lips again.

"Oh, baby," Sheila said against her mouth. "You kiss me like yes."

"I mean yes."

Rushed, as if revealing more than she was used to, Sheila went on, "There are women who want to come and skip the kisses. They think that if I don't kiss them, the fuck doesn't count somehow. But you . . . I want it all. I want to kiss you, hold you. And make you come because that's what you want. Me, making you come. That's the yes that really matters."

"I do want that, Sheila," Erika said shyly. "Nobody's ever put it that way before."

"I want to be sure . . ." Sheila swallowed, her eyes suddenly shadowed. "I want to be sure you mean yes because, oh honey, I've wanted you for a couple of years now."

"Years?" Erika nearly laughed. "Even when we were still in college?"

"Yeah."

"Even when you were working the late shift at Mickey D's?"

"Yeah."

Erika couldn't help but tease. "Does this remind you of the time you were working the late shift at Mickey D's?"

Sheila lifted one eyebrow lazily. "Yeah. There was this night when I cleaned out all the grease—"

178

Erika kissed Sheila, quick, hard. "Touch me, baby. It's what I want to do with you, right now. And, later, if you want . . ."

Breathlessly, Sheila said, "We'll talk about later, later. God, you're so wet."

Erika stiffened against Sheila's fingers as they rippled against her soaked panties. "Kisses, it's those kisses."

She wrapped her arms tight around Sheila's shoulders as those deft, playful fingers teased her through the sheer fabric. "I want to make you scream."

"Yes," Erika moaned.

"Fuck your brains out. Sometimes I'm evil, and I can't get enough." Sheila was smiling, but her obvious delight was also edged with wonder. "Will you come for me more than once?"

"If you want me to. I'll come all night." Sheila's fingers felt like fire. "Please, please fuck me."

Fingers immediately pulled her panties aside and pushed inside her. "Like this?"

It was a moment before Erika could breathe. "Yes. Oh, Sheila. God, yes."

"I want you naked, now." Sheila was already on her feet, pulling Erika up with her. "Everything off and you on the bed."

The poms were already lost on the floor somewhere, and Erika stripped off her sweater and miniskirt as she followed Sheila to the bedroom. Sheila was unfastening the chaps and shedding the rest of her clothes too. When Sheila peeled down her boxer shorts, Erika shyly removed her Wonder bra and matching panties.

Abruptly, they were both naked. Erika's heart was pounding so hard she felt almost unreal. When Sheila pulled her close for another long, wet, searching kiss, she crumpled. In moments, Sheila had lowered her to the bed.

"That's right. In the middle." The dim light that reached them from the living room cast Sheila's face in shadow, but Erika wasn't afraid. She could hear the soft edges of Sheila's voice echoing in her heart where she'd been holding in so much feeling for so long. "Show me yourself."

Sweeping her hands along the inside of her thighs, Erika lifted her hips. Sheila lit a candle and the flare of the lighter illuminated her dark eyes, which sparkled with arousal.

"Is this what you wanted to see?" Erika parted her lips and trailed her fingers over her cunt. "You want to see how wet I am? How ready I am?"

"Yes, baby, that's exactly what I want." Sheila shuddered with a deep breath. "Do you have any idea how hot you're making me?"

"I hope it's as hot as you make me. I'm soaked. I want you." She pushed two fingers into her cunt and could hardly feel them, she was that wet.

Sheila made a noise, something like the breath having been knocked out of her. "God, let me do that."

Erika looked up at Sheila, now leaning over her, and took in the sharp lines of her face and the tangle of her hair and felt Sheila's fingers ease inside her. No longer buddies. They were lovers. Finally on the other side of their longing, Erika wanted to capture the richness of the moment. It would take work to stay in love, to keep passion like this hot—

"Fuck, you're so wet. God, my hand's getting lost. I didn't know you were so open, baby."

Erika tried to find her wits. "What was I supposed to say? Hey, Sheila, pretty sure you could fist me without lube?"

Sheila groaned. "I probably could. Damn, you're so . . . wait, wait, baby, relax."

Erika paused in the arc of lifting her hips, realizing her only goal had been to try to take Sheila's hand inside her. "Please, Sheila, please—"

"We're using lube. I'm not going to hurt you, not the first time, not ever. I want to do this all night."

180

Erika watched Sheila scrabble in her bedside drawer. She could feel her cunt swelling as the throb of desire grew more intense. "You don't need it. I can tell."

"Oh, yeah?" Sheila had a bottle out now, and slowly drizzled some the length of her forearm. "You have no idea how hard and how long I'm going to fuck you."

Erika had no words left. As Sheila leaned over her, she grasped Sheila's elbow, pulling her in.

"All at once? No, baby, like this. Four fingers," Sheila said through gritted teeth. "God, that's easy. I want to fuck you a little like this. Nice and easy. Like that?"

Erika nodded as she gripped Sheila's arm harder. She loved it, but couldn't find the words to say so.

"Nice and easy and . . . all the way in now."

Full, she was full. If she could have breathed, Erika knew she would have screamed. Sheila felt fantastic inside her, rolling her fist, then moving up and down a little, then deeper.

"Oh, fuck, you are so open, baby." Sheila closed her eyes and Erika was stunned by the look of awe on Sheila's face.

She wanted to be special and different, magnificent and unusual, not like anything Sheila had ever felt before. And that look said maybe she was . . . maybe.

Sheila opened her eyes and the look, for just a moment, was again overflowing with a tenderness that brought tears to Erika's eyes. Then Sheila put her head on Erika's stomach.

She pulled her hand out, pushed in again and Erika arched wildly. Sheila's other arm went around her waist just as Erika clutched her shoulders, digging her nails into the muscles there.

They moved together until their bodies were slick with sweat, until Sheila needed more lube and Erika once again greedily pulled Sheila's hand into her body.

"I didn't know you were wild," Sheila breathed into her ear.

"With you," Erika managed to say, the first words she'd spoken since Sheila had plunged inside her. She wanted to say so much more, explain about trust and not fear, about desire and longing and all the fantasies, but it was all too complicated when Sheila was pushing the inside of her wide open.

"You're so beautiful, inside, like this." Sheila was panting and they kissed wildly, shaking sweat off their faces and tears from their eyes.

Words, too many words, Erika thought, then she realized Sheila was right. It was really very simple. She found the breath somehow, and said hoarsely, "Make me come."

Sheila bared her teeth in a fierce grin. "I thought you'd never ask."

The shower felt heavenly. Erika was pleased that Sheila's legs appeared to be as wobbly as her own when they emerged from the steam and dried each other off.

"I love you, you know."

"I know that now." Sheila toweled her hair, then wiped stray drops from Erika's chest. "I don't know what I was afraid of. I don't know why I wasted these past few years when we could have been doing that the whole time."

They shared a shy, dopey-feeling grin, and Erika liked what she thought she saw in Sheila's eyes.

"Your eyes are really expressive."

Sheila tipped her head back to comb her hair with her fingers. "Yeah? What are they saying?"

"They're saying that we just had fantastic sex and you'd like to do that again sometime soon."

Sheila lifted one eyebrow. "Anything else?"

"You can't believe we finally did it and how good it really was."

"And?"

Emboldened by the golden glint in Sheila's eyes, Erika added,

"That you want to sleep late tomorrow and then let me make love to you, and if that goes well, fuck my brains out."

"Is there more?"

Expecting to be tickled, Erika added, "Your eyes are saying that you worship the ground I walk on and will make me breakfast in bed and intend to go on loving me for a very long time."

"Know what?"

Erika draped the towel over the nearest bar, then let Sheila pull her into her arms. Safe, loved, warm. "What?"

Sheila ducked her head, then glanced up through her lashes, so shy and vulnerable that Erika thought her heart would break. She put one finger under Sheila's chin to lift it. Their gazes met, locked.

Erika asked again, "What?"

The smiles were gone, leaving only tenderness. Softly, Sheila said, "What you see in my eyes is true."

The Works

"Do you have a couple of quarters?"

Why my lover decided to stop to get the car washed I had no idea. But I dutifully fished in my clutch for a few coins. Butches don't carry a lot of pocket change. It ruins the lines of their jeans—and they insist that femmes are vain. I pushed aside tissues, compact, mirror, brush, cell phone and finally reached my coin purse. "Here, I have three more."

"Great. I only had nine."

Okay, so she carried change, but I was annoyed we were getting the car washed. I really wanted to hurry home from the party where Mary had been driving me to distraction all night. Now she was driving me through a car wash, at *midnight* I might add, like grime on the tires was more important than my needs—needs that she had made more intense with all the kissing, hugging, smooching and flirting. Okay, so it was thirty miles to home and the tank was low, but did we have to get a wash, too? Why had she dragged me into our hostess's bathroom for several minutes of making out and feverish groping if we were going to stop for gas?

She looked so hot in that James Dean hairdo, white T-shirt

and a fake pack of cigarettes rolled into her sleeve. I had thought my teensy-weensy black skirt, thigh-high fishnets and sleeveless crushed velvet mock turtleneck—not to mention the kitten ears and claw-tipped gloves—had been successfully driving her insane with lust.

More than a little peevish, I observed, "A tank of gas plus two bucks for the Deluxe Wash is what I usually get."

Mary eased the car forward into the dark enclosure until the light turned red. The water whooshed on and the windows were instantly wet. She carefully put the engine in neutral and set the parking brake before she said, "True, but for an extra dollar you can get the Works."

Before I could do anything more than squeak she unfastened my seatbelt and pulled the handle to drop my seat back nearly horizontal. Her lips were at my throat and then all of her was on top of me.

I loved the feeling of denim against my thighs. "Baby!"

"You've been making me crazy all night with that costume and knowing you're wearing that little lacy nothing-of-a-bra underneath." She yanked my top up and expertly unsnapped the front hook. Her mouth found each nipple in turn, teeth rasping over them. "I want to devour you whole."

"Do you see me putting up any kind of fight?" My surprise quickly turned into heat. Even though we were cloaked by water, machinery and darkness, I was exposed to her in the car and, damn, it turned me on. I'd never guessed just how much it would.

Her hand was under my skirt, fingers digging into my thong. I'd been wet most of the night, thanks to her endless teasing, and now I was sodden. I relaxed into her kiss, her touch, with a welcoming moan.

"No, baby. No time for that that sweet, easy stuff. I want to do more than pet the sexiest kitten in this entire city." Mary kissed me hard as her hand pulled my thong down.

"Honey, not here—"

"Yes, here. Right now. God . . . oh you're *soaked* . . ."

Her fingers sank into me, then played with my lips and folds as they slipped up and down the length of my cunt.

"Of course I am." I paused to catch my breath. "You've been teasing me all night."

Another set of sprayers passed over the car, leaving the windows streaked with multicolor foam.

"Spread your legs, baby, come on, let me fuck you." She nibbled my lower lip and her hand teased my opening. "We've only got another two minutes for the Works."

I started to laugh, but she went inside me, and it felt so good—and so naughty—that I groaned.

"You don't have to be quiet, come on, baby. Feels good doesn't it?" She had that cocky impish butch look on her face as she eased her fingers out of me slowly. Every muscle in my cunt gripped at her, trying to keep her inside. "I don't know why it's taken me so long to fuck you in the car. I think we both like it. And tonight you're my favorite kind of cat."

"Pussy," I managed to say.

"My pussy." Her fingers slammed into me and all in an instant I was open, very open and dripping wet. I was only dimly aware of the heavy brushes rocking the car. We were adding a rhythm of our own. I was momentarily scared that we'd roll out of the building and into the street, then remembered she'd set the brake. I rocked up against her. "Fuck me, then. Fuck me hard."

"That's right, I'm fucking this hungry, wet pussy of yours." She bit down on my nipple, then rubbed her lips over it. "You're so wet I could shove my fist inside you—"

"Oh, baby." The thought of it brought up my hips with my fuck-me stiletto sandals braced on the dash. I wanted to tell her how crazy she was making me, but all I could manage was another shrill, "Oh, baby!"

"We'll do that later. I'll fuck you inside out later. All you have to do right now is come for me."

I wound my gloved, claw-tipped fingers into her thick hair, ruining her style for the night, and she moaned. The windows were sheeted with water and the last of the bubbles were gone. She fucked me, and fucked me, deeper and deeper and I couldn't believe how close I was to coming. She was massaging exactly the right places, but it was more than just her touch. It was the suddenness of her seduction and the hot, wicked lust in her eyes.

A loud thump signaled the end of the last rinse and the wax sprayers whisked over the car. Her palm bumped my clit every time she pulled out of me, then her fingers sinuously found every nerve that had ever responded to her touch as she pushed back in.

The sprayers finished, but I wasn't sure that I could. It was too quick, but my cunt felt so good. Just a few minutes more, and I knew I'd come.

The dryers came on and began their slow pass over the hood. I fancied that I could feel the heat, only it was from the inside where the friction of her fingers was melting me. Muscles dissolved.

"That's right," she said hoarsely.

"So good. God, that's so good." I wanted to stay tight against her, give her all my strength to match hers, but my legs were going limp.

Low in my ear, she said, "When we get home I am going to fuck you on the floor in the kitchen. Then the table, it's been forever since I had you on the table. I'm going to strap it on for you—"

"Oh, baby!" I twisted my claws in her hair as my mind snapped with images of her when she gets this way and how I always respond.

"Strap it on for you and fuck you against the wall in the hallway. It'll be hours before we get to the bed." After a groan, she added, "When we finally get there I'm going to fuck you all over again."

The dryer finished with the windshield, but the night beyond the car wash was a blur to me. Her knuckles were pushed nearly all the way inside me. I was so close.

"And then my sweet little kitten is going to have to eat me—"

"God."

"Get settled between my legs and lick me for a long—"

"Oh, fuck."

"Long, long time. Oh *yeah*. That's it, you're there, come on, baby, give me everything. Come all over my hand."

Her words flipped the switches. I was pulsing and tight and yet open, I had to be open to let it go, to come for her, scream when a second wave hit me. Then her mouth was on mine and we shared a frantic, wet kiss that promised a night neither of us would soon forget.

The dryers retracted as she collapsed into the driver's seat, gazing at her wet hand. I'd had no idea I could come that hard, that fast.

"I think," I said shakily, "that the Works was worth the extra dollar." I was surprised that the heels of my sandals hadn't left marks on the dash.

Eyes half-closed, she sniffed her fingertips.

Collecting my wits, I leaned over to lick her coated fingers just to hear her groan. I wiped her hand on my breasts for good measure and pulled down my shirt.

"Oh, leave it up, honey, I love the way you look half-naked."

"I'd prefer not to get arrested. What would you have done if I hadn't had three more quarters?"

"Fucked you faster."

I burst out laughing as my whole body clenched in sensuous delight.

She gave me her smug, lopsided grin. It delighted me to see it, because without me she wouldn't get to strut like that. I strut in my own way, reveling in her disheveled hair and the tremor in her arms. And I was perfectly aware that she was temporarily rapt as she watched my fingers smooth over my still soaked, still slippery lips.

I speculated that nobody could see below my waist in the dark. Maybe I'd leave my skirt up for the drive home to see just how high I could spike her pulse.

She released the parking brake moments before the light changed to green and flashed *Exit Carefully*.

"If you have the time," she said, oh so seriously, "always get the Works."

Come Hither, Woman

~1A~

Ace stomped on the last empty beer can. "That was our best party ever."

"I can't believe we don't even have some pretzels left. I'm starving." Neenah trailed tiredly into the bedroom. At least there was nothing to be cleaned up in there. Last year they'd discovered that some guests had obviously used the bed and had been forced to change the sheets. It had to have been the Tramp-Who-Shall-Not-Be-Named, Ace's ex. It was the kind of nasty trick she'd pull. "I just want to soak my feet and call it a night."

"I'm right behind you."

"Promises, promises." She kicked off her soft, comfortable moccasins and headed for the bathroom. Once the tub was filling, she carefully got out of her faux deerskin dress and met Ace in the doorway.

"You were the most beautiful woman there tonight." Ace took the time to kiss her properly, as she always did.

"Next year," Neenah said, "you have to wear a proper costume. No more name badges."

"What's wrong with this one?" Ace pointed to her *Demonics R Us* employee card. "This year I made supervisor."

"Goof." Neenah kissed Ace back before hanging up her dress. The unfortunate incident with the guacamole earlier meant it was headed to the dry cleaners.

"So, do you think Carmen and Joyce had a private party?" Ace tossed her jeans and polo shirt into the hamper.

"Well, they took off out of here like there was no tomorrow. I hope so. They're both nice."

"Yeah, that's why I introduced them. They talked for a long while, and I don't think they noticed anybody else the whole time."

"Parma and Willow never came back either."

"Did you do that? Invite Willow?"

"Yeah."

"You love to matchmake."

"Willow did her part. I just gave them a chance to get acquainted again." The water was just right, and Neenah lost no time easing herself into the tub. She closed her eyes, but moments later felt splashes across the surface of the water. Her nose told her what it was before she got her eyes open. Fizzy rose crystals, her favorite.

She gave Ace a dreamy look. "Thank you, sweetie. That's wonderful."

Ace winked as she put the jar back on the shelf, then resumed brushing her teeth. Neenah was tired in her bones from standing for hours. Meanwhile, Ace looked as if she could do it all over again—that was what pulling double shifts and spending ninety percent of her job on her feet did for her stamina.

Her eyes nearly closed, Neenah let herself enjoy the sight of Ace bent over the sink. Fine-boned, firm-muscled, a little more plush in the tummy than ten years ago when they'd met—all that was true. But in every inch of Ace's body, every change, wrinkle and gray hair, she could read the history of their relationship.

"What?" Ace had looked up from the sink while Neenah drifted in her thoughts.

"I'm just enjoying the sight of you. You look as if you could have partied until dawn."

"I never lock my knees. It makes a huge difference."

"So you say. I can't remember."

Ace bent over to smooth her toes. "I've got a nail that's chipped. Oh, yeah, it's right there."

Watching Ace fetch the clippers, Neenah felt the familiar swell of tenderness for the simple richness of their life. How could anyone think sharing the little things was boring when she loved all the details that made Ace the woman she was? All around her it seemed as if people fell in and out of love with rapidity, but she was just as in love with Ace's brash, boisterous being as she'd been all those years ago, trying to come up with excuses to visit the doctor so she could chat with Ace again.

It wasn't a long journey from Ace's heels to her knees, but Neenah took her time, tracing the hard calf with her gaze until it gave way to the soft skin behind the knee. She smiled, recalling all the times she'd kissed her way along the journey, stopping to nibble at the softness. Ace's fit of giggles and pleas for mercy from the tickling always broke the mood, but they recaptured it so easily, and laughter was always good for the soul.

If I weren't so tired, Neenah mused. Ace's inner thighs were smooth and yielding. A gentle touch of Neenah's hands had never failed to part them, leading to hidden wonders. She knew that Ace had half her coworkers believing they had the kinkiest sex life in the city, but it wasn't often that Ace wanted more than Neenah's attentions at that sensitive, responsive spot. Their love was that simple, that intense and that pleasurable.

"What's that look?" Ace had again caught her staring.

"I was thinking about your thighs."

"Oh, really?" Ace turned toward the bath. "And what did you conclude?"

"That I love spending time between them."

"And I love that you do."

"I'm really glad you're a woman." Neenah stretched to touch Ace's belly. "Every bit of you."

"Me too. I'm fond of the machinery. Most of it, anyway, about twenty-four days out of every month."

Neenah's hand slipped down until she could coil a curl of Ace's pubic hair around one finger. She tugged slightly. "Have a bath with me."

"I thought that was the look I was getting."

"What look?"

"Come hither, woman."

Neenah pursed her lips. "Can you read me that easily?"

Ace slid into the other end of the tub, tucking her knees up and avoiding the faucet. "You're an open book to me."

"Well, if that's so, what are you doing facing that way? Come hither, woman!" Neenah squealed as Ace's immediate obedience sloshed water on the floor. "Goof."

They nestled into the hot water, Ace turned in Neenah's arms so they could kiss as they talked.

"I am really tired," Neenah admitted. "But you are looking pretty good to me tonight."

Ace blushed. It amazed Neenah that, after all these years, a statement of desire could make Ace turn so wonderfully red.

"I don't know what all I can manage, but . . ." Neenah leaned down to whisper in Ace's ear. "But tasting you is high on the list."

"Geez, Neenah, are you trying to give me a heart attack?"

"Yep. You're insured, after all."

Ace tickled her, which turned into more languid, loving kisses. Eventually, Neenah made token wipes with the washcloth and Ace shampooed them both. The water was starting to cool when they clambered out.

"Thank goodness tomorrow is Sunday."

"You said it." Neenah welcomed the warmth of her ratty green robe as she padded to the bedroom.

"If you're too tired . . ."

Neenah threw a sleepy but wicked glance over her shoulder. "Come hither, woman."

"Okay." Ace plopped on the bed and waggled her eyebrows suggestively.

"Let's see . . . I think given that it's the witching hour we need . . . a magic wand."

Ace laughed and reached for the cord. As she inserted the plug into the outlet she observed, "A magic wand with variable speeds is a good thing."

"You." Neenah pointed. "Over there. Your side of the bed. I'm putting you to sleep."

"What about you?" Ace's smile lost some of its vibrancy as she gazed at Neenah slipping off her robe. "I'd love to put you to sleep."

"I'll need no help tonight. In." Neenah pulled back the covers. She watched Ace settle back on her pillow, then slowly, gently, settled on top of her lover's warm body. "Tell you what," she murmured. "Why don't you wake me around noon?"

"Oh, honey." Ace pulled Neenah into her. "It'll be the best damn brunch you've ever had. If there were Olympics for sex, they'd find a way to ban us."

Kisses had always been so easy and so good that sometimes Neenah forgot all about having sex. But not tonight, she thought, even as Ace nibbled and kissed and loved her mouth. Her eyelids drooped. Oh lord, she wasn't going to fall asleep, was she?

Ace's hands stroked her back and then gently squeezed and massaged her ass. She wanted to burrow and purr. "Oh, that feels good."

"Mmm-hmm." Ace looked far too lively. "Why don't you straddle me, baby?"

"Uh-uh," Neenah protested. "I'm putting you to sleep."

"Sure you are."

"I am. Here, have a vibrator."

Ace laughed as she maneuvered the cord so neither of them was laying on it. "Honey, you don't have to."

"Tell me you're not jazzed from all that dyke energy."

"Well, I am, true."

"So . . . a little relief?"

Ace was still grinning. "I'm not nearly in as bad a shape as Mary's girlfriend. I thought the poor kitty-cat was going to explode."

"Mary was being really bad. And don't change the subject." Neenah settled to one side of Ace, within comfortable reach of Ace's always welcoming right nipple. One little nuzzle and sure enough, it said hello. "Look at that. My, my. Your mouth may say no, but Girl-on-the-Right says yes."

Ace blushed slightly as she fumbled with the vibrator. "Oh, okay. Hell. Fine."

Neenah smiled as she toyed with the deliciously firm tip. They both giggled when the headboard light dimmed slightly, then Ace stiffened against her. Neenah loved that feeling, the way arousal swept over Ace like a wildfire. "Feel good?"

"Yeah," Ace said, her voice tight.

Her hand languidly traveled the length of Ace's torso. "I don't suppose you'd like me to help you out, would you?"

"Don't tease, Neenah. This isn't going to take . . . long." Ace arched slightly as she dug her toes into the bed.

Careful not to bump the vibrator—once Ace found the right spot it was now or never—Neenah slipped her hand between Ace's thighs. She played with the silky hair, still damp from the bath, until her fingers found the kind of wet that Neenah loved to play with.

"Don't tease," Ace repeated. "Please, Neenah."

With a little moan, Neenah pushed one finger just inside Ace, who went rigid. "You feel really good tonight."

"Just like that," Ace panted. "Just . . . like . . . that . . . Neenah! God!"

She wrapped Ace tight in her arms through the shudders and the aftershocks, some of which were as long and strong as the original climax. Ace finally went limp and Neenah was amused and pleased to see her eyelids droop.

She put the vibrator out of reach—nothing like waking up with an appliance in one's back—and switched off the lights. The streets outside were quiet, finally, and as she drifted to sleep herself she focused on the only sound that really mattered: the even, steady rhythm of Ace's breathing.

Up on the Rooftop

Rooftop

~Part 3~

Suze is putting everything back in her pack, though I still don't know what to say. Abruptly she looks up and catches me staring. "We're going to go, right?"

I nod. Go where, I want to ask. Is our Halloween evening over?

"Amy? Are you okay?"

No, I want to say. No, I haven't been okay since that day you said something over your lunch and laughed and the world starting spinning backward. "What do you want to do now?"

Suze gives me a wide-eyed look. "Take you back to my place and ravage you, of course."

I know I am supposed to laugh, but I can't.

Suze's smile fades. "Sorry, that was crass."

"No, the costumes with the, uh, things hanging out, that was crass."

"I thought the dildos were cute."

Nobody in Iowa ever said *dildo*. I'm pretty sure if anyone did, they'd burst into flames. I can't say it. I feel gauche.

"Amy? What's wrong?"

Where do I start? "I told you I was gay."

"Yeah. I knew, but I'm glad you told me."

"Do you like me?" The words are out before I can stop them. My heart's flopping around on the rooftop.

"Sure," Suze says immediately. "You're fun."

Fun. Like a sister? Like a pal? "I've been called worse, I guess."

"I mean it," Suze says. "You were scared to crash the building with me, but you did it. And we've had a good time tonight, haven't we?"

I nod, remembering the sights glimpsed through the windows across the street. They were having fun too. I want to be that kind of fun. Really fun. I look across the street, but the only lights on in the building are the ground floor. Then they wink out, too, and it feels as if the party really is over.

Suze sounds odd when she asks, "Would you like to get some early breakfast? I know a diner we can walk to. Might be crowded. We might have to wait for a table."

"Okay. That sounds like fun." I don't want the night to end. I can still hear *dildo* and *ravage* in my head and my heart won't stop beating fast.

"Forget what I said, earlier." Suze slings her backpack over her shoulders and doesn't look at me.

"What?"

"About . . . ravaging. I didn't mean . . ."

I think I'm going to cry. I blew it. I should have said yes. I blink really hard to hide the tears.

"Do you like *me*?" Suze leads the way to the stairwell. "I've never been quite sure."

"Yes, Suze. I like you. You're fun too."

She nods. Looking shy, she takes my hand and we stare at each other. "I'm glad you like me. That was brave of you, to ask me that."

I don't know what to say. Her hand is so warm and skin to skin is how all of my fantasies about Suze start. "I wasn't sure."

"I'm not the ravaging type," she says abruptly.

"Oh."

"So when I said . . ."

She's still holding my hand, but she's not looking at me.

Amazed, I ask, "Are you blushing?"

"Maybe."

"I don't know if I'm the ravagable type, so, it's not like I could say yes."

"If you were and I were, would you say yes?"

I sort through the hypotheticals and think I know the right answer. "Yes."

Suze looks at me again, her eyes sparkling. "Sure you say yes, but what was the question?"

"Do I want to make out with you and see if we end up in bed after some breakfast?"

Suze lets out that delighted shout of hers. "Yes, that was the question. You Midwesterners cut to the chase on everything."

"No, we don't. We avoid everything. I've been trying to tell you for ages that I'm gay. I think I'm just blossoming in some California sunshine."

"Do we have to wait until after breakfast?"

"For what?"

She squeezes my fingers. "Silly. To make out."

"Oh." I bite my lower lip.

"Is that a yes or a no?"

I realize then that if I say yes, Suze will kiss me. I really want her to. I don't feel much like the old Amy anymore. I want to make it permanent. I'm not Amy from Iowa any longer and I want to shed her like a costume that has served its purpose. I'm Amy, lesbian, San Franciscan. I spent Halloween in the Castro.

She's waiting for my answer. It's amazing the power I feel

right then, like I have never known before what I want and how to get it. Never felt that all I had to do was reach out for my dreams and they'd be there right within my grasp.

If I say yes, she'll kiss the old Amy. I'm the new Amy, forever more.

So I kiss her.